Lectures on M. Renans Vie De Jesus

SALZWASSER
VERLAG

John Tulloch

Lectures on M. Renans Vie De Jesus

1st Edition | ISBN: 978-3-75258-254-3

Place of Publication: Frankfurt am Main, Germany

Year of Publication: 2022

Salzwasser Verlag GmbH, Germany.

Reprint of the original, first published in 1864.

LECTURES

ON

M. RENAN'S 'VIE DE JÉSUS.'

THE CHRIST OF THE GOSPELS AND THE CHRIST OF MODERN CRITICISM:

LECTURES

ON

M. RENAN'S 'VIE DE JÉSUS.'

London and Cambridge

1864.

PREFATORY NOTE.

These Lectures were written during last winter in Rome, for the use of my Students in St. Andrew's. Compelled by ill health to leave the active discharge of my duties in the hands of others, I felt, with returning strength, reluctant to be idle in my professional capacity, even amidst the engrossing glories of Rome. My attention had been drawn to M. Renan's volume before leaving home. It encountered me in all my wanderings in the Mediterranean and Levant in the early winter. It was everywhere a common topic of conversation. Many minds were evidently disposed to accept it as a satisfactory explanation of Christianity. Many more did not know very well what to think it, but were disposed to regard it as a very significant, if not altogether successful, attack upon religion and the Church. I thought I could not do better than write a few lectures upon it.

Some friends in Rome, knowing what I was about, asked me to read the lectures; and they were read there to successive companies of friends, chiefly clerical—American, Anglican, and Scotch-Presbyterian—whose intelligent criticism I recall with pleasure.

To myself these few lectures must always have something of a mournful interest, associated as they have been with a time of painful trial and suffering. At such a time one learns to look within, to see on what his life is resting. Christianity is nothing to me or any man, if it is not a source of living strength—"the light of life." This, I trust, I have found it to be in a time of need. And out of the fulness of my feeling I have spoken—very imperfectly, I am aware—it may be weakly, according to the convictions of others, below what they may feel and realize of Divine Truth; but honestly according to my own convictions, as I have always sought to do.

Grave, however, as are the faults of M. Renan's work, and unworthy as appears to me the spirit animating certain parts of it, I have not felt called upon to indulge in any denunciation of either. To all personal criticism in such discussions I have a strong aversion. It never does any good, and it is in itself a mean and contemptible weapon. In a time like ours, when Christian

Truth needs so much the advocacy of reason as well as of zeal, it is painful and sad to think how the cause of this Truth sometimes suffers from a mode of advocacy inconsistent not only with Christian principle, but with those rules of honourable courtesy towards opponents which now prevail in all higher circles of intellectual activity.

I may add that I have not seen Dr. Strauss's new and popular work on the "Life of Jesus," and that all my remarks, so far as he is concerned, of course apply to his previous well-known work.

CÆPRI, *May.*

CONTENTS.

V.

VI.

I.

The publication of M. Renan's "Vie de Jésus" marks a crisis in the present course of philosophical and religious opinion. This is its chief significance. The book itself has been judged very differently, from different points of view—denied all merit by some—loudly applauded by others; but the grave import of its appearance, and of its immediate wide-spread circulation throughout Europe, cannot be questioned by any. It has caused a greater shock in Christen-

Note.—The references are, throughout, to the fifth French edition.

dom than any work since Dr. Strauss's "Leben Jesu," while the attractiveness of its form and style has already given it a reputation and an influence far more extensive than its more elaborate German predecessor. In England, and throughout the Continent, it is a common topic of conversation. It is heard of amidst all the excitements of political, and of military struggle; in the halls of Oxford, in the *salons* of Paris, in the churches of Italy, in the counting-houses of the Levant. While we write, it is the subject of solemn "reparation" services in all Catholic countries, and the Archbishop of Smyrna, Apostolic Vicar of Asia Minor, has just published a "Pastoral" to his Clergy, in vindication of the Faith against its daring statements. It is indispensable that students in divinity should know something of such a work, or rather—for no student can be kept ignorant of it—that they should be able to say something regarding it, not merely by way of deprecation and condemnation, but of intelligent appreciation and reply.

Like its German predecessor, the "Vie de Jésus" marks the spring-tide of an advancing wave of thought inimical to Christianity. As the former was the result of Hegelian speculation, and of the crisis reached by rationalistic criticism, the natural consummation of the anti-Christian activity of the German intellect through many years; so the work of M. Renan is the result, and, it may be hoped, the consummation, of the course of materialistic thought—known as Positivism—which since then has been active, not only in France, but in England, Germany, and elsewhere, and of an historical criticism divorced from all faith and true reverence. So far there is a remarkable analogy between the works. They are the respective types of a definite mode of anti-Christian thought.

In other respects they do not present much resemblance. The "Vie de Jésus" is a more dangerous, but, so to speak, a less formidable book. It is more dangerous, because it addresses a far wider class of readers; it is designed to influence the young and the multitudes of educated and half-educated minds in our day, who are impelled by the atmosphere of inquiry surrounding them, to investigate such a subject as the origin of Christianity, but who have neither the resources nor the leisure to investigate it thoroughly. It is less formidable, because less solid, and apparently less earnest. In these qualities the German work is greatly superior. In the language of German theology the "Leben Jesu" was acknowledged to be a strictly scientific treatise, addressed to theologians and mainly aiming at their enlightenment and advance. With comparatively few attractions of manner and style, it is throughout grave, philosophical, and vigorously polemical, presenting an array of argument and learning far more imposing than the light and rapid pages of the present work.

But the chief difference in the influence of the two works, will be found to arise from the different modes of thought which they represent, and to which they appeal. Neither Hegelian philosophy, nor rationalistic criticism in its successive developments, strangely exciting as they were in Germany, created much excitement beyond Germany. The former has remained to this day an esoteric system, unknown save to a limited circle of speculative students; it is said to have been abandoned or idly regarded by Dr. Strauss himself in after years. Positivism, within the last quarter of a century, has become an active, and even fashionable mode of thought, and nowhere more so than amongst certain literary and intellectual circles in England. So far as it is a philosophy, it is adapted to the common understanding, and falls in fitly with the scientific and social tendencies of the time; while it has received a noted impulse from certain living writers of great ability.

But Positivism is, characteristically, not so much a definite philosophy, as a method of philosophising, — a way of thinking about science, life, and religion. And this way of thinking largely affects many who know little or nothing of M. Comte's particular opinions, or who may not even have heard of M. Comte himself. There is no one who knows anything of current literature, either French or English, who does not know that the influence of Positivism has in this manner extended widely, and prepared, as it were, for the reception of a work like M. Renan's, which should apply its principles and modes of reasoning to the Gospels and the Life of Jesus.

This state of intellectual preparation, combined with the genuine literary merits of the "Vie de Jésus," is sufficient to account for its extraordinary circulation, and the remarkable interest which it has excited everywhere. There were waiting, so to speak, for such a book, many minds stored with vague novelties as to the growth of religious and social constitutions, and the general development of civilization, such as Positivism suggests, and groping in that dim perplexity of spiritual inquiry which is so common in our time. A volume which professes to account for the origin of Christianity, and to explain the appearance of Jesus on ordinary historical principles, within a few hundred pages, written in a charmingly facile style, and with an apparent depth of thoughtfulness and sentiment, could not fail to secure hosts of readers, and to excite universal attention.

Some critics, we observe, have turned the extremely popular character of the work into a reproach against it. They allege that a book of such a character places itself beyond the pale of grave theological discussion; that it is more a romance than anything else, and scarcely deserves serious refutation. Even Dr. Ewald, of Göttingen, who would be supposed by many in England to be a fellow-worker with M. Renan, is reported to have denounced the volume as conceived and written in a spirit unworthy of theological science. But whether such a reproach be deserving or not, we cannot help thinking that it is an unhappy device of Christian theology to despise and overlook any book, evidently influential, on such a ground. It would seem as if in certain quarters the old antagonism between Christianity and literature in its more attractive forms, still lingers. There are good people who seem to imagine, that a book cannot be at once very pleasant and very valuable. Dulness has its prescriptive rights; and a certain heaviness of thought and style is supposed to be peculiarly suitable in theological discussion. Gravity certainly always becomes such discussion. But even if the "Vie de Jésus" should appear to us lacking in appropriate gravity, it would be absurd to satisfy ourselves with neglecting and disparaging it merely on this account; for it is its very literary attractiveness, its clear beauty and fluency of style, its confident gaiety and piquancy of argument, the ease, lightness, and rapidity with which it moves along through all the difficulties of its subject,—the imaginative brilliance which lights up its descriptive sketches, and the glow of sentimental enthusiasm which is but seldom wanting in its moral discussions, which give to it its peculiar influence, and make it at once so seductive and so dangerous to many minds.

Nor, we confess, much as we shall find occasion to condemn M. Renan's tone, do we see any reason to doubt, upon the whole, his honesty of intention in this, or in any other of his works, which are mostly devoted to Biblical or religious subjects. In all of these works he seems animated by a spirit of inquiry, which, if tinged by a pervading materialism, and something of the careless, sensuous ethics of his country, is yet, in its way, thoughtful and sincere. He is deeply interested in the historical origin and development of religious opinions; and to the investigation of such topics he has brought the resources of a rare, comprehensive, and living learning. Of this latter point there can be no question, whatever we may think of the application he has made of his learning in the present case, particularly of those extravagant pretensions, as to the Talmud, by which he has sought to cover the weakness of his position, and to impose upon himself and others. His scholarly acquisitions he has further improved and vivified by residence in the East, and intelligent personal contact with Eastern manners and institutions; while to his other qualifications he adds that fine turn for generalization, so characteristic of the critical and historical intellect of France, and which gives to all its productions a rare charm for educated readers.

There is really no point of view, therefore, in which M. Renan can be conceived a weak or contemptible opponent, or in which his volume does not demand and require the awakened attention of the Christian theologian. In this conviction these lectures have originated, and as they have been written in some degree to satisfy the writer's own mind, as well as discharge a formal duty, they may be found helpful to guide and inform the minds of others.

I. M. Renan's book first demands our attention in its philosophical aspect. It is the expression, we have said, of a prevailing philosophical tendency. Its fundamental and controlling conception takes its rise in a system of thought very marked at the present time. This fact is apparent on the face of the volume. The author not only does not conceal, but throughout the introduction and early chapters, parades, the great Positivist idea *of an unchanging material Law governing all things, the world of history, as well as the world of matter.* And in certain passages he expressly appeals to this idea as the necessarily guiding principle of all historical investigation,—and of the investigation of the origin of Christianity, no less than other historical problems,—in the very same manner as Strauss appealed to certain Hegelian conceptions, and sought to bring Christianity within their conditions. He tells us, as a matter of course, in one of his earliest pages,[1] that the "Gospels are partly legendary," for the reason that "they are full of miracles." Any miraculous relation is to him incompatible with historical veracity. It is enough to stamp a record as so far fictitious or legendary, that it acknowledges the reality of the supernatural, or incloses any professed miraculous occurrences. And this, he contends, is not to impose any preconception or theory upon history, but simply to insist upon the critical observation and analysis of facts. "It is not in the name of this or that philosophy," he says,[2] "but it is in the name of a constant experience that we banish miracle from history. We do not say that 'miracle

[1] Introduction, p. xv. [2] Ib. pp. l. li.

is impossible,' but merely that no miracle has been hitherto proved." "None of the miracles with which ancient histories are filled, have happened under scientific conditions. Uniform observation teaches us that they only happen in times and countries where people are prepared to believe them."

We shall afterwards have occasion to consider what he says on the special subject of "scientific conditions," applied to a miracle, and to examine the value of his supposed tests or conditions. In the meantime we wish to fix attention upon the general principles of his philosophy, rather than their particular application. He would have us to understand, from the above statement, that he, and the school to which he belongs, are free from theoretic bias in the interpretation of historical facts. But this is just what it is impossible to concede to them. *They are theorists*, and of a most extreme character, in their views of history, and their explanation of some of its most characteristic phenomena. M. Renan may pretend not to affirm the impossibility of miracles—merely to judge them from a critical and historical point of view; but such an affirmation is in the face of the whole spirit and scope of his book. It is contradicted almost in the very breath in which he utters it. For why should recitals of miracles be necessarily legendary[1] if miracle be not held to be *à priori* impossible? On what ground, otherwise, are the Gospels at once pronounced to be partly legendary? For observe, this is said antecedent to all examination of the Gospel miracles, or their appropriate evidence. "No miracle has been

[1] Introduction, p. l.

hitherto proved!" Is not this to beg the whole question in a spirit of arbitrary theory? For what but such a theory can cover an affirmation of such sweeping generality.

But we are not left to mere inference for M. Renan's theoretic views on this subject. In another and very striking passage—striking both in itself and in its connexion—he enunciates them with the utmost plainness.[1] The passage is found in the chapter on the "Education of Jesus"—a chapter singular in its vague, bold, and unauthorized surmises. He describes the rustic simplicity in the midst of which Jesus passed His youth in Galilee, as a quiet villager, loving the country, and having no taste for the artifices and pomps of contemporary greatness. Of the imperial world

[1] Pp. 30—43.

surrounding Him, the youthful Son of Mary had evidently no just conception. The earth seemed to Him divided into kingdoms that made war one with another. The "Roman peace," the "Roman power," were to Him merely vague conceptions. The name of "Cæsar" alone had reached His ear. The imposing architectural works of the Herods in Galilee and its neighbourhood He regarded with displeasure. All He loved was the sweet Galilean country, with its artless villages, its clusters of lowly cottages, and gardens, and wine-presses hewn out of the rock, its wells, tombs, fig-trees, and olive-trees. "He remained always near to nature. The court of kings was to Him only a place where people lived arrayed in fine clothing." And while the youthful Jesus was thus ignorant of the contemporary events and circumstances of His time, He knew still less of its philosophy and science. The great idea of Greek science, the basis of all philosophy, was unknown to Him—the idea, namely, that the government of the world is by universal laws, and not by capricious deities. "Nearly a century before Him"—and we now translate directly from M. Renan—"Lucretius had expounded, in an admirable manner, the principle of the inflexibility of the laws of nature. The negation of miracle, the idea that all proceeds in the world by laws in which the personal intervention of superior beings has no part, were truths held in common by the great schools of every country which had received Greek science. Probably even Babylon and Persia were not strangers to them. But Jesus knew nothing of this progress. Although born in an epoch in which the principle of positive science was already proclaimed, He lived in the full consciousness of the supernatural. Never, perhaps, had the Jews been more possessed with a craving after the marvellous. . . . In this respect Jesus differed nothing from His compatriots. He believed in the existence of the Devil, whom He regarded as a sort of evil genius; He imagined that nervous maladies were the result of demon-possession. The marvellous was not exceptional to Him; it was the normal condition of His life. A man ignorant of physical law, and who believes that he can by prayer change the course of the weather, and arrest disease, and even death itself, finds nothing extraordinary in a miracle. The whole course of things is to him the result of the free volitions of Deity." Such a man was Jesus. Such was the intellectual state of Jesus.

Here there can be no doubt of M. Renan's philosophical sentiments, and as little doubt of the manner in which he applies them to history. It is his evident principle, as it is that of the whole school to which he belongs, to ignore the reality of any spiritual or Divine government of the world. The order of the universe is fixed in certain laws, which exclude all personal intervention, and remain unchanging for ever. It is the business of science to discover these laws; it is the function of the historian to recognise their operation, and to interpret by them the whole course of past phenomena; for it admits of no question that they are the same laws which we now see operating around us, which have been, without deviation, operating from the beginning. There is, and can be, no room, therefore, in history for miracle. There is no room even for God, save as the poetic or philosophic ideal of an inflexible system of law. This is Positivism in its general conception —the startling creed of a widely prevailing philosophy. Not only Christianity, but Theism is held to be a philosophical mistake. The world has not advanced—nay, has retrograded from the days of the great schools of Greek science. It is the spirit of Lucretius, the recognition of his "inexorabile Fatum," which is the highest point of wisdom, and to which the world must return as the spring of its higher progress and the consummation of all knowledge.

It is somewhat hard for the Christian apologist, to be thus continually dragged from the fair field of historical evidence, to a discussion of the ultimate principles of all truth. And yet it is a very instructive fact, that every school of unbelief is now driven to this resource. It makes its chief attack upon Christianity from behind general principles, not merely inimical to the Church, and the supernatural foundation upon which it rests, but inimical to all religion; inimical, in fact, to all spiritual philosophy, and every noble creative art and product of civilization which has its root in the spiritual life of man—the sphere in which man is allied to a higher divine life than the mere nature around him, which he can see and handle. For this is the real question involved in Positivism. It is not, as writers like M. Renan ingeniously put it, a question between law and caprice, order and arbitrariness in the government of the world. There is no Christian thinker who believes that the government of the world is otherwise than by general laws. The universe of nature is conceived by all reflective minds as a great order or *cosmos*, and the course of history, apparently irregular as it has been, as a consistent development in the great system of things. The Theist recognises the principle of *order* quite as plainly as the Positivist; but what he does not admit, is, *the merely material character of this order.* He maintains on the contrary that order is everywhere the direct expression of a living Divine will, which rules in and by the order. He acknowledges, equally with the Positivist, that the material facts or phenomena in the midst of which he lives are capable of classification into general laws, continually subsisting, and of which they may be regarded as the issue or manifestation; but he does not allow that these material phenomena, or their laws, exhaust the realities of being. On the contrary, he holds that the highest being of man is not contained in them, but is a part of, and is closely allied to, a higher order of being, transcending and embracing the other. Every higher activity of our nature presupposes and springs from this higher order of being. Religion has no meaning apart from it. Philosophy, as it has been conceived by all the highest minds of the human race—by a Socrates or a Pascal, or even by a Pythagoras, or a Kant, has no basis without it. Art of every kind, poetry, painting, and sculpture, imply, and appeal to it; and, save for the inspiration they draw from thence, would be merely the toys of an idle and frivolous luxury. Civilization, in its legislative and judicial institutes, and in all the more characteristic and elevating forms of its manifestations, rests upon it, grows with its growth, and decays with its corruption. That man is something more than matter, that there is a Divine Spirit in him, and a Divine Spirit above him, in Whom alone he lives; and that this Divine order of Being is higher than the mere material order, and may for wise and beneficent purposes supersede and traverse this lower order; that, in short, there is a living Supreme Will, directly governing all things, and communing with, and controlling the will of man; an Almighty and Personal Hand, which "none can stay from working" —such a faith is indeed eminently Christian. But it also lies, more or less obscurely, at the root of every form of religion, and every conception of man as a being capable of rational and moral progress. And this is what Positivism, if not in all cases expressly, yet in its essential character implicitly, denies; for it acknowledges nothing higher than Nature, and the system of laws into which Nature may be resolved.

Such a Philosophy—if Philosophy it can be called—necessarily excludes all idea of miracles. It ejects the miraculous from history because it has already ejected God from the world. Let it pretend as it may not to impose theory upon history, it does so in the most obvious and sweeping manner. For why are miracles incredible?—not because they have been examined and found to be devoid of credit—but because the world proceeds by general laws and not by personal agency. Deny this latter fact, and of course no miracle can have ever happened—for a miracle in its very idea presupposes personal agency. But admit the reality of a Divine Intelligence and Will governing and acting in every manifestation of nature and of history, and it is impossible to exclude the idea of miracle, or at once set it aside. For if there be a Divine Intelligence and Will moving all things, and moving man, of which man is a sharer, how may they not manifest themselves directly to man? What is there then inconceivable, still less improbable, in the supernatural? Is not the Divine, or supernatural, the reality, the substance, of which Nature, the material, is only the shadow? And may not miracle, in its true conception, as brought before us in the life of Christ, and origin of Christianity, take its right place in the development of the world's history, as a direct manifestation of the Divine for human good; as the stretching forth of the Almighty hand, not by way of interference, still less of disturbance, but for the purpose of urging forward in a more powerful and consistent manner the wheels of the world's progress. *May not miracle be a fact of this kind?* We do not meantime take higher ground, and it is not necessary to take higher ground to upset the pretensions of our author's Philosophy. Surely we are entitled to this modest surmise! For how imperfect and dim after all must be our conceptions of the highest order,—how little can we be entitled to erect our little generalizations into exhaustive and universal canons! What poor judges must we be of the possible or impossible in the realm of God! We do not dare to assign bounds to the possibilities of history, or to apply our theories without reserve to the ways of God. All this Positivism does in its essential principles. Is it not enough to say of any philosophy, that it denies God and dishonours man? Taking away from the former all personality and freedom of action—from the latter all soul, all life beyond nature: degrading the one into a blind fate, the other into mere matter.

Whatever may be the rights of such a philosophy, it cannot have any claim to stand at the door of history, and to determine for us its laws, and the character of its facts. For let it be borne in mind that M. Renan does not offer a single word in vindication, or even in formal exposition of a theory by which he at once shuts out the miraculous from history, and God from the world which He has made. He does not profess to argue in its behalf; he simply announces it as the ultimate philosophy. The Gospels are partly legendary, because they are in part records of miraculous occurrences. The pretensions of a pseudo-philosophy cannot go further. We are at least entitled to hold our own position against such an insolent demand to surrender. Surely it is not the Christian apologist who is here the dogmatist. He believes in God, it is true, but he does not venture to accept the Christian miracles without inquiry and evidence. M. Renan at once rejects them without inquiry, because he has no faith in a living God, and no faith in the Divine government of the world.

II.

We have endeavoured to explain the philosophical significance of M. Renan's volume. It comes from the mint of French Positivism, just as Strauss's equally famous and more elaborate work came from the mint of German Pantheism. Any criticism which fails to apprehend the speculative origin of these remarkable works will, so far, fail to understand them. Strauss sought to turn the Evangelical history into a series of myths, because he had already confessedly adopted a speculative system inconsistent with the idea of the veracity of this history. The history must be false, or at least mythical, because, according to him, the notion of a Personal God and Creator of men, and of a Son of God revealing the will of a Heavenly Father, is *unphilosophical*—a dream of superstition, and not a truth of reason, as expounded by its latest and highest prophet, Hegel. In the same manner, M. Renan denies the veracity of the Gospels, in part, because they are inconsistent with his philosophical conception of the government of the world by law. The notion of a Personal Will interposing in human affairs is incompatible with science, which, according to his view, teaches, with irresistible force of evidence, that the order of the universe is unchanging. It is the speculative error, therefore, which is the fruitful and germinant error in both cases; and we must be prepared to encounter such false philosophies by a Philosophy at once more modest and more comprehensive. We must be ready, from the bosom of a higher thought, as well as of a deeper faith, "to give a reason for the hope that is in us." It may seem a wearying process to be obliged thus continually to go back to the "principles of the doctrine of Christ," and to lay over again, as it were, the "foundation" of our religion; but it is a necessity from which no student can well escape. A religion that is not philosophically grounded, in a time like ours, must feel constantly weak in presence of the persistent attacks made upon it by philosophical weapons which it does not understand, and the real strength of which may be either greatly underrated or greatly exaggerated, according to its ignorance.

A clear and thoughtful comprehension of

the principles of Theism must be the best and the only adequate means of meeting the unbelief propagated by such works. It is not enough merely to learn those principles, or gather them from others; but we must sift them, and make them our own in the depths of our spiritual and rational experience, until we feel that the instincts which connect us with a Personal God and Father in the heavens are a true part of our very being—deeper and more real than any other facts in the universe, and having, therefore, a philosophical or rational groundwork, in comparison with which the most imposing philosophical theories are mere illusions, incapable of moving us. Such a vital experience of the rational consistency of Theism and of the harmony of its truths with the deepest study of nature and of history, and with our profoundest insight into the mysteries of this complex being, will be found the best safeguard against the seductive generalizations of writers like M. Renan. He denies miracles because he does not believe in a Supreme Will governing the world; because the idea of *material law* has swallowed up, with him, all idea of *free moral volition*. We believe miracles, on the contrary—or, at least, the miracles of the Gospels, because the reality of a Supreme Will, directing the world and moving in all the affairs of men, is a paramount dictate of our rational consciousness—a truth which asserts itself equally with the truth of our own personal existence; and because the expression of this Will, or *a moral Providence*, is to us not only a higher conception than that of *material law*, but a conception which embraces the latter, and without which it has no meaning and no reality. We are utterly separated, therefore, in thought, as well as in faith; and "miracle" is not only not impossible to us, but already intelligible in the sphere of our reason and the light with which it invests the manifestations of nature and the "ways of God to man."

Where there is such an opposition of thought in regard to the Supernatural, it may seem of little use to enter into more detailed discussion of M. Renan's views as to miracles. But on the same ground we might decline controversy with him altogether; and this would be neither a useful nor a courageous course. The Christian theologian need not provoke controversy, but he is not entitled fairly to decline it, and, disengaging himself from contact with an evident enemy, to pass by on the other side. When the conflicts of doubt and of faith are so incessant and perplexing as in our age, and when they penetrate into all classes of society and all channels of intellectual and literary intercourse, it is far better to come out to the enemy and meet him at every point. Truth has never anything to fear in such discussion, but receives new confirmation from encounters with every novel and ingenious fallacy which seeks to pervert it.

Such a result seems to us particularly illustrated by our author's further statements as to miracles, and the tests or conditions which he would apply to them, and we now proceed to consider these statements. After telling us that no miracles have " hitherto been proved," he goes on to tell us what sort of proof he desiderates. The passage in which he does this is the only piece of argument which he offers on the subject; and the argument has evidently appeared to himself as somewhat original and convincing; for he has repeated and dwelt upon it with pleasure in the Appendix to the famous Inaugural Lecture which occasioned his dismissal from the University of Paris, and which he afterwards published in explanation and justification of his conduct. The passage, therefore, invites our consideration; and all the more, that the consideration of it involves the important question of *evidence* touching miracles, and the Christian miracles in particular. Nothing can well be more important than to have a clear and just conception of the nature of this evidence, and of the conditions within which it claims our assent.

M. Renan's argument must be stated in his own language: "No miracle," he says, "has ever been performed before an assembly of men capable of verifying the miraculous character of a fact. Neither common people nor people of the world are fitted to do this. It requires great precaution, and a long habit of scientific research. Have we not, for example, in our time, seen society become the dupe of coarse pretences or puerile illusions? Miraculous facts, so-called, attested by whole villages, have disappeared before a more rigorous inquiry, as utterly worthless. And if it be thus proved that no contemporary miracles bear discussion, is it not likely that the miracles of the past, which were all performed in the presence of mere popular witnesses, would be found equally illusive if they could be subjected to the same careful scrutiny? . . . Were a worker of miracles to present himself in these days, with pretensions sufficiently serious to be discussed, and to announce himself, we shall suppose, as capable of raising the dead, what should we do? We should appoint a commission, composed of physiologists, physicians, chemists, and persons trained in historical criticism. This commission would choose a dead body; would assure themselves that it was in reality a dead body; would select a room for the experiment; and arrange an entire system of precautions necessary to place the result beyond doubt. If, under such conditions, the raising of the dead was effected, a probability nearly equal to certainty would be obtained. However, as an experiment must be always capable of repetition—as those who have once done a thing must be able to do it again, and there can be no question of easy or difficult in regard to miracles—the miracle-worker would be invited to reproduce the miraculous fact in other circumstances, and upon other dead bodies, in another company. If on each occasion the miracle succeeded, two things would be proved: first, that supernatural facts happen in the world; and, secondly, that the power of producing them belongs to, or is delegated to, certain persons. But who does not see that no miracle has ever been performed under these conditions; that the miracle-worker has always himself hitherto chosen the subject of experiment, and the company or witnesses before whom the act was to be done; more frequently still, perhaps, that it is the people themselves—obeying an invincible impulse to recognise something Divine in all great events and great men—who have created, after the event, the miraculous legend or story. Historical criticism, therefore, compels us to maintain it as a principle, that recitals of miraculous events are, *per se*, inadmissible; that they always involve credulity or imposture, and must consequently be sifted and explained to see how much of truth, how much of error lies in them."[1]

Such is M. Renan's argument. Let us look at it for a little. Miraculous facts must be scientifically tested—This is the purport of the argument. But is not this in the nature of the case an absurd and impracticable test? Does not the very idea of such a test raise a different question, and imply a fact of an entirely different order from that of a miracle? Let us take an

[1] Introduction, pp. l.—lii.

example; and we willingly take one suggested by M. Renan's language.

Our Lord, in the course of His journeys, went into the city of Nain, and as He went, ("and many of His disciples and much people went with Him,") He met a funeral procession, with the dead body of a young man, carried on an open bier, according to the custom of the East, and his weeping mother following the bier. "And when the Lord saw her, He had compassion on her, and said unto her, Weep not. And He came and touched the bier, and they that bare him stood still. And He said, Young man, I say unto thee arise. And he that was dead sat up and began to speak, and He delivered him to his mother. And there came a fear on all. And they glorified God, saying, That a great Prophet is risen up among us, and that God hath visited His people." Think of this scene—a touching and memorable incident—one among many, although few so striking, in the life of our Lord. Then recall, for contrast, M. Renan's laboratory, and assembly of scientific commissioners prepared to investigate the alleged resuscitation of a dead body, carefully selected and scientifically scrutinized. The contrasted facts are of an entirely different order, and the issue contemplated in the one case is quite distinct from the issue alleged in the other.

The Widow of Nain's son—was he raised from the dead or not? It is perfectly fair to put this question. The fact admits of inquiry, and of proof if it happened. But what sort of inquiry, and what sort of proof? Scientific inquiry, demonstrative proof, says M. Renan. Not in the least we say. The *nature of the fact* is inconsistent with this kind of inquiry and evidence. The raising of the Widow of Nain's son, if it really took place, was an historical fact, and as such it has nothing to do with scientific experiment —the tests of repeated trial and demonstration do not apply to it. It belongs to a different category, and rests on evidence quite distinct.

M. Renan has here fallen into so plain a confusion as to confound a fact of experience, a professed historical incident, with a scientific conclusion. *Facts of incident or contingency*—and all historical facts, miraculous or otherwise, are of this class—belong to a sphere of their own—different from the scientific—and rest on their own characteristic and appropriate proof. Whether *anything has happened* or not, is a question of contingency to be settled by the evidence of those who profess to have seen the thing happen. Did they really see it? Were they truly cognizant of it? And were they capable of judging—not by scientific tests, but by the ordinary exercise of their senses and their judgment—whether what they saw was a reality, and not an illusion? Are they honest men, and have they no inducement to say that the thing happened, if it did not happen? Such is the nature of historical evidence. Scientific evidence is of a different character; the evidence not of personal testimony, but of continual demonstration as has been already described. Scientific facts, unlike facts of mere contingency or incident, are truths of nature which, once discovered, admit of repeated verification, because they rest on the constitution of things—the existing laws of the material universe; they are equally true at all times therefore, and their proof can be demonstratively exhibited at one time as well as another. In the case of such facts, personal evidence is of no consequence. No amount of such evidence, apart from scientific experiment and demonstration, could establish, for example, the law of gravitation, or the law of equilibrium of fluids. You or I may believe these scientific truths, because of Newton's statements on the one hand, or Pascal's statements on the other; but any number of such statements does not form the *appropriate evidence* of such truths. They rest, on the contrary, on the evidence of direct observation and experiment, capable of constant repetition, and of being exhibited in formulæ of the utmost exactness and certainty.

M. Renan asks with triumph, Who does not know that no miracle has ever been performed under the conditions laid down by him? May we not ask, with a more justly-founded confidence, Who does not see that a miracle, performed under such conditions, would be no miracle at all? So soon as you can reduce any fact within scientific laws and conditions, it necessarily ceases to have the character of a *miracle*. It is the very idea of miracle, that it transcends these laws and conditions; that it is an incident or occurrence, appearing within the sphere of human experience, but incapable of being resolved by the ordinary laws which govern this experience. If it can be so resolved, it loses all pretension to be miraculous, or even marvellous. And so it is that many pretended miracles have been exploded by an explanation of the natural principles or laws of operation under which they have been produced. If the case supposed by M. Renan could really occur, the conclusions which he draws from it are not those which would really follow. The true inference would be, not that miraculous powers have been entrusted to certain persons, but that raising the dead was a natural or scientific process, and not an exhibition of miraculous or supernatural power at all. How could it be, if capable of spontaneous repetition in the manner suggested? For is not this capacity of repetition just the characteristic of a scientific fact? Is not the process described the very process by which some new truth or law of science is discovered and verified? A miracle, on the other hand, implies, as its essential idea, a special and extraordinary exercise of Divine power, which, from its very nature, it is absurd to suppose repeated with a view to verification.

It pleases God Almighty, let us suppose, with a view to man's good and the demonstration of His own glory, to interpose in human affairs, arresting the ordinary action of the laws of nature—as in the case of immediate recovery from sickness, or restoring the dead to life again. The operation of the natural forces which make up the course of human experience, and which only subsist at any moment because God, who appointed them, continues them, is temporarily set aside for some wise end, so that the Original Will—of whom alone all these forces are, and whose power alone they express—is made bare, stands forth, as it were, in direct demonstration and authority. This is the Christian idea of a miracle—*the will of God in direct and extraordinary exercise.* This is the nature of the fact which M. Renan insists upon calling together an assembly of scientific persons to settle. Is this the hand of God? They are to determine the question by experiment, and by an application of scientific tests. If the hand of God raises a dead man to life, it must repeat the process under a more rigorous and vigilant scientific scrutiny, before the scientific notables can determine whether the thing has been really done or not. It is surely needless to add, that no miracle has been hitherto performed under such conditions; for the conditions entirely divest the supposed act of all Divine character—nay, of all moral import. The idea of God repeating an exercise of His will for the gratification or information of an assembly of *savans*, is surely one of the most preposterous—might we not say blasphemous?—ideas that could have occurred to any mind.

For historical facts, or facts of incident, there can only be the evidence of *personal testimony*—no other. Did an alleged fact happen yesterday, to-day, a hundred, or a thousand years ago, how can we learn whether it happened or not? By carefully examining the evidence of those who profess to have witnessed the fact. If their evidence is satisfactory, if it stands the tests we are bound to apply to it, as to the honesty and competency of the witnesses, we are bound to accept it; or, at least, if we reject it, we must reject similar evidence in other cases; in short, we destroy the foundations of historical credibility. And, essentially, the case is not altered by the alleged fact being a miracle. Was the widow of Nain's son raised from the dead? Was Lazarus restored to life again after having lain in the grave three days? If we allow such facts to be capable of proof at all, they can only be proved by evidence of the same kind as certifies the fact that Julius Cæsar was slain in the senate at Rome on a certain day of the year 44 B.C., or any other equally admitted historical occurrence.

It is very true that, in the case of a professed miraculous occurrence, other considerations, besides the mere amount and value of the personal evidence, must come into view, and at times so prominently as to render almost unnecessary the consideration of the alleged evidence. In order to establish a miracle, it is by no means enough that we have a host of honest-minded people saying that they saw such a thing at such a time. To this extent M. Renan's scepticism is perfectly justifiable. If we were told, for example, by some twelve grave and honest people that they saw a man on a given day or night ascend to the roof of a room, and float suspended in the air without any apparent support, we should not, perhaps, distrust their testimony, or say that they meant to deceive us; but we should, nevertheless, refuse our assent to their story. We should not believe that any man did what they say he did. And the case is no imaginary one in a time like ours. Whatever might be the apparent strength of the evidence here, we could not believe it; and why?—not simply because the alleged fact contradicts the laws of nature (M. Renan's plea against all miracles)—but because while it does contradict the laws of nature, it does so with no serious intention, with no moral, not to say, no beneficent aim. It bears the stamp of falsehood on its front—meaning nothing, accomplishing nothing—a notable instance of human folly.

Here the principle "Nec deus intersit" at once comes into play, and may serve to settle the matter without looking at the evidence at all.

It is impossible to separate miracle, in any case, from general considerations as to the character of God and His government of the world. For what is miracle, according to our frequent definition, but the special action of God—the extraordinary manifestation of the Divine Will; and how can we therefore separate it from the thought of God and the apparent designs of His will in nature and in providence? To suppose an aimless or absurd miracle is to suppose an impossibility.[1] A faith that would accept miracles

[1] Still more a "moral miracle," as suggested by an Oxford writer in certain well-known Bampton Lectures. The conception of a "moral miracle" is an essentially sceptical conception which can only be vindicated on

without Divine meaning is a faith without reason, and for which we do not venture to plead.

In the case we have supposed, therefore, we refuse our assent to the alleged fact at once and conclusively. We know that the twelve witnesses have been deceived in some manner, although we may not be able to explain in what manner. We know that men do not float suspended from the roofs of houses, nor spirits give answers to foolish questions, notwithstanding that hundreds may tell us that they have seen the one and heard the other. They may have done so. We do not question their honesty nor yet the evidence of their senses, though both may be truly liable to question. But

grounds which would destroy the moral tests of credibility, and so sap the foundations of religious belief altogether.

we know, nevertheless, that they are mistaken. For the very reason that God is God, and the laws of His universe divine laws, we know that He does not reveal His will after this manner.

What M. Renan says with reference to legends we may say with far more truth of miracles: *There are miracles—and miracles.* There are occurrences in the past, professing to be miraculous, that must perish before the advance of historical criticism, which spares not anything, and is not bound to spare anything, that it can really explain. Such occurrences, from shining large and mysterious to our early imagination, must "fade into the light of common day," and disappear in its full blaze. But there are other occurrences, and the miracles of the Gospels among them, which shine all the more radiant, full and significant, the more they are examined. Let the light be turned upon the mere marvel or portent, it vanishes; but these witnesses of Divine love and power, these symbols (σημεῖα) of an infinitely beneficent meaning, only stand the more firmly in the face of any philosophical and historical method which is reverent as well as keen, inductive as well as subtle, which is faithful, in short, to the moral instincts as well as the intellectual impulses of humanity.

III.

But it is now time to turn to another aspect of M. Renan's volume. From its philosophy, we proceed to consider its criticism. There is an obvious connexion between the two; the latter is greatly influenced by the former, as in Strauss's case; but the "Vie de Jésus" does not boast any such comprehensive and consistent critical method—exactly adapted to the exigency produced by the author's philosophical system—as the "mythical theory." The exigency is of this kind: the Gospels are not to be accepted as historical narratives—true in every part, or even in the main, like other histories.

The miraculous recitals are in their nature un-historical. The question then comes—what explanation do they admit of? Are they to be regarded as having any claims upon our belief? Are they in any degree historically credible?

In reply, Dr. Strauss presented at least a very intelligible and consistent answer. The idea of the Myth as a characteristic element in the early history of all peoples was, at the time of his studies, rising into notice. The critical mind had grasped its importance, and recognised, with a kind of creative joy, how widely applicable it was, and how well it served to account for the highly-coloured story of all infant civilizations, and the heroic supernatural aspects which they assumed. The answer of Strauss accordingly was—the Gospels are in no degree historically credible. But neither are they fictitious, still less false, in the ordinary sense. They are not the impositions or inventions of any sect with a view to deceive the world, as the older forms of Rationalism inclined or permitted to believe. The mere progress of historical study had entirely exploded that notion. But they are a collection of myths, the spontaneous and unconscious growth of the Jewish imagination in the beginning of the Christian era. The only historical nucleus of the whole is the name and personality of Jesus, dim and uncharacteristic,—a Jewish Rabbi, who had gathered around Him a number of followers whose faith and hopes He had greatly excited by His preaching, and the power and charm of His manner. All the details of the Gospels, miraculous and otherwise, were the creation of the marvellous excitement thus kindled in a few minds, and breaking forth into objective representation and story. The narratives of our Lord's birth—of the visit of the Magi—of His youthful appearance in the Temple—of His baptism, temptation, and "beginning of miracles" in Cana of Galilee—of His preachings and wonderful works in the villages around the Lake of Tiberias—of His Paschal journeys and conflicts with the Pharisees—of His tender touching interviews with His disciples in His last days—of His passion, resurrection, and ascension—all, in short, that rises before us the grand, living, most human yet most Divine, image of the Gospels, were the idealizing pictures, and nothing more, with which the Galilean imagination in a trance of creative enthusiasm had surrounded the name of Jesus. They were the embodied dreams of a few Jews raised to a height both of practical heroism and of imaginative hero-worship by the long-inherited traditions of a baffled and self-concentrating patriotism. As the Hellenic imagination created circles of ideal activity around heroic names; or as the more narrow Latin imagination conceived those patriotic idyls with which it tried to deceive itself, and so long deceived the world, as to the origin and progress of Roman greatness—so did the Jewish imagination produce the Gospels, and impose them upon human belief. The incidents of the Evangelical History are not really more historical than the exploits of Perseus and Hercules, or the legends of Virginia and Coriolanus.

Such was the famous mythical theory. It has perished, like the previous theories of the "vulgar Rationalism" which it superseded. There is no historical student in our day would urge it as equal to the exigency which it proposed to meet—as furnishing, in other words, a complete and satisfactory explanation of the phenomena of the Evangelical History. But, as a theory, it had at least the advantage we have hinted—of consistency and comprehensiveness. Attributing all the Gospels more or less to the same cause, it supposed that they gradually sprang up as the Christian tradition gathered force and deepened in dogmatic intelligence, and that none of them consequently, in their present form, ascend to the first Apostolic Age. In what way they originated and were moulded into their present shape amidst the conflicts of the time, it has been the aim of the well-known Tübingen school of Sceptical Theology to show.

M. Renan does not profess any such comprehensive critical theory. He is complimentary indeed to Dr. Strauss, and commends the influence of his labours; but his own historical studies, and the mere progress of historical knowledge, if nothing else, prevents him from adopting any similar explanation of the Gospels.[1] He makes little or nothing of the mythical theory, although its influence may be plainly traced in many parts of his work. According to him, the Gospels are one and all to be regarded as the productions of the first century. He does not even except the Gospel of St. John, as we shall find, although his views regarding this Gospel are very wavering and difficult to fix. The following is his account of the origin of the several Gospels.

First, he supposes that there were two primitive sources of Evangelical tradition,

[1] Strauss's detailed criticism of the text of the Gospels, he says, "leaves little to be desired. But he is wrong in his theory; and his book, according to me, has the disadvantage of keeping too much on theological, too little on historical ground."—Introduction, p. viii.

corresponding to the discourses or *Logia* of St. Matthew, and the anecdotical narrative matter of St. Mark. He believes that the expressions of Papias, in the well-known passage preserved by Eusebius, favour, and indeed demand, this supposition; and he repeatedly recurs to his interpretation of these expressions, and urges it upon his readers. We shall afterwards consider how far he is justified in this, by a special examination of the passage. But, in the meantime, we proceed with the explanatory statement of his views.

Following out this idea, he supposes that the documents mentioned by Papias, are the nuclei of our present Gospels of St. Matthew and St. Mark. Gradually these primitive nuclei of the Evangelical tradition passed into more elaborate composite forms. The manner in which this transition took place marks the second stage in the history of the Evangelical narratives. It is impossible to do justice to our author's theory on this subject, except in his own language. "The early Christians," he says, "cared little for any written accounts of the sayings or actions of Jesus. As they believed that the end of the world was approaching, they only cared to preserve in their hearts the living image of their Master about to appear in the clouds in glory. The evangelical texts, accordingly, acquired little authority during the first half-century of the Christian era. No scruple was felt in supplementing, combining, and completing them from different sources and from one another. The poor man, who had only a single book, naturally wished it to contain all which touched his heart. The Christians borrowed, accordingly, from one another these small books, and each transcribed on the margin of his copy the touching words or parables which he found unknown to him before. The most beautiful result in the world was in this way the issue of an obscure and entirely popular elaboration"! Is there not an unconscious irony in the language? Thus arose our present Gospels of St. Matthew and St. Mark—"impersonal compositions," bearing no trace of individual authorship ("*ou l'auteur disparait totalement*").

The third stage in the history of the Gospels is that of individual compilation, represented by St. Luke. The Gospel of St. Luke is "a regular composition, founded upon anterior documents. It is the work of a man who selects, adapts, combines;" a work "at second hand," in which the words of Jesus are set forth more reflectively and with greater arrangement. M. Renan makes no doubt of this Gospel being really the production of St. Luke, the companion of St. Paul, and the author of the Acts of the Apostles. Here, then, we have a definite production of the first century,—following very soon the destruction of Jerusalem, in the year 70,—genuine in every sense. But the historical value of this Gospel, he proceeds to say, is the least of all. It represses details with a view to produce an artificial agreement; it softens passages which might prove embarrassing to the growing ideal of Christ as divine; it exaggerates the miraculous, and commits errors in chronology. The author is entirely ignorant of Hebrew, and does not cite any of the words of Jesus in that language. To all the Jewish localities he gives Greek names. St. Luke, in short, is a harmonist and compiler, who uses liberties with his texts, and does not scruple to bring them into a forced accord.

The fourth and final stage in the origin of the Gospels is, of course, the stage of speculation and conscious narrative purpose, represented by St. John. This Gospel is supposed, also, to have been in existence in the end of the first century, or the very beginning of the second. The statements of Justin and his contemporary apologists, Tatian, Anixagoras, and Theophilus of Antioch, along with those of Irenæus, place this beyond question. M. Renan even inclines to regard the Gospel as in part, at least, the work of St. John himself. He hesitates greatly, and changes, apparently, his standpoint and his conclusions as they suit his immediate purposes. But his predominant view is, that John, in his old age, having read the other Evangelical narratives, and marked their deficiencies, and being moved, moreover, by some feeling of offence that he had not received a sufficiently prominent place in these narratives, began to dictate to his disciples his own impressions and reminiscences of the life of our Lord; and that these brief notes of their master were afterwards elaborated and supplemented by his disciples. He does not pretend, however, to have any clear idea how far this process of revision and addition extended. This and other difficult questions concerning the fourth Gospel could only be "settled by some insight into the events of that mysterious school at Ephesus which more than once appears to have delighted to wrap itself in obscurity." But in whatever degree the fourth Gospel may have been the work of the disciples of St. John rather than himself, it is of capital value as an authority regarding our Lord's life. Any one setting himself to write this life without a preconceived theory as to the relative value of the Gospels, and following the guidance merely of the sentiment of the subject, and its natural development, would be led, in a multitude of cases, to prefer the narrative of St. John to that of the Synoptics. M. Renan, in short, values the Gospel of St. John for its historical accuracy, and disparages it for its discursive doctrinism. The language he uses on the latter subject must be as strange as it is painful to many Christian students. How often have they been moved by the sublime and pregnant discourses of the fourth Gospel, thrilling with a fulness of Divine revelation which at once satisfies the soul and draws forth all its powers. To our author these discourses are nothing but long egotistical argumentations, wanting in life, freshness, and force!

There is one point, in particular, on which he has bestowed great pains and elaboration. The tone and doctrine of the fourth Gospel, he says, are quite inconsistent with the tone and doctrine of St. Matthew, so that we cannot accept both as a true representation of Christ. We must make our choice between them. "If Jesus spoke according to St. Matthew, he certainly did not speak according to St. John. And between the two," he continues, "no critic can, or will, hesitate. If even Papias had not told us that Matthew transcribed the words of Jesus in their original form; the natural, the ineffable truth, the matchless charm of the synoptical discourses, their profoundly Hebrew cast, the analogy which they present to the sentences of the Jewish doctors of the same age, their perfect harmony with the natural features of Galilee—all these traits, in comparison with the obscure gnosis and metaphorical monotony which fill the discourses of St. John, point alike to the same conclusion. This does not imply that there are no admirable glimpses in the discourses of St. John—traits which come directly from Jesus. But their mystical tone in no degree corresponds to the eloquence of Jesus, such as we picture it to ourselves in the other Gospels. A new spirit has breathed—the gnosis has already commenced; the Galilean era of the kingdom of God is finished; the hope of the new coming of Christ is distant; we enter among the aridities of metaphysic—the obscurities of abstract dogma; the Spirit of Jesus is not there; and if the son of Zebedee has really traced these pages, he must have forgotten, while he did so, the Lake of Gennesareth and the delightful conversations which he had heard upon its banks."

So confidently does M. Renan express himself. The result of the whole is that, according to him, the Gospels contain elements of history, but nothing more. They are not mere fictions, conscious (according to the old infidel view) or unconscious (according to the modern mythical view); but neither are they credible historical narratives throughout. As he himself puts it, they are neither biographies after the manner of Suetonius, nor merely fictitious legends after the manner of Philostratus. "I should compare them rather to the legends of the Saints, the lives of Plotinus, of Proclus, and of Isidore, and other writings of a similar kind, where historic veracity and the intention of presenting models of virtue, combine in different degrees. The inaccuracy, which is a feature of all such popular compositions, makes itself particularly felt." And in illustration, he supposes the modern parallel of two or three old soldiers of the Empire, who might undertake the task of writing the life of Napoleon from their recollections. There is no parallel too audacious or startling for M. Renan, if it only appear to his vivacious fancy to give piquancy to his pages. These old soldiers, he says, would make all sorts of mistakes in the narrations — would reverse the order of their hero's exploits, and would omit some of his most important expeditions altogether; but they would, one and all, probably preserve a high degree of truth in the single matter of the character of their hero, and the personal impression which he made upon them." In this respect "popular histories are of much more value than solemn and official history. We can say as much for the Gospels. Solely bent on setting in relief the excellence of their Master, His miracles, His teachings, the Evangelists show an entire indifference to all which is not of the same spirit as Jesus. Contradictions as to time, place, and persons, are regarded as quite insignificant; for while we attribute to the words of Jesus Himself a high degree of inspiration, we are far from according the same inspiration to the Evangelical editors. These we must regard merely as scribes, having one aim in view—to omit nothing which they themselves know.

"Beyond contradiction, some preconceived ideas must mingle themselves with such recollections. Several naratives, especially of St. Luke, are plainly invented to bring into more lively relief the portrait of Jesus. This portrait itself would undergo a change day by day. Jesus would be a unique phenomenon in history if, with the part He played, He had not been very greatly transfigured. The legend of Alexander was already in full play before the generation of his companions in arms had died away. That of St. Francis of Assisi commenced in his lifetime. A rapid work of metamorphosis proceeded in the same manner during the twenty or thirty years following the death of Jesus, and imposed upon His biography the rounding touches of an ideal legend. Death perfects the most complete Man. It exhibits him without stain for all who loved him."

We must postpone to another lecture

our special examination of M. Renan's views as now presented, and the grounds on which he supports them. But there are certain general considerations by which in the meantime we may fairly judge the character of his criticism.

(1) And, first of all, it deserves to be noticed how entirely *subjective* his method of criticism is. The Gospels of St. Matthew and St. Mark, he says, cannot be received as original in their present shape; they are evidently collections, or miscellanea, and not the definite productions of single minds, as they have descended to us. The discourses of the one, and the lively, anecdotical matter of the other, are the only parts stamped respectively with originality. Saving the obscure hints of Papias, which we shall find do not warrant his interpre-

tation, he does not profess to give any proof of these statements, nor does he seem to think that they need proof. So the matter appears to him. And in the same spirit, and even from a more subjective point of view, does he deal with St. Luke and St. John. He speaks of errors in chronology, of forced agreements, of exaggeration of the marvellous, of ignorance of Hebrew on the part of the former, without assigning anything that can be called proof. He gives a few references, nothing more, but these references, which we have been at the trouble to verify, are absurdly inadequate and inapplicable. Not one of them, it may be said, does not admit of an interpretation inconsistent with that which he puts upon it. And this, we shall find, is especially true of the oppositions of thought and doctrine which he tries to fix between St. John and St. Matthew. These oppositions are in great part the creation of his own brain, proceeding from his determination to keep out of view what does not suit his purpose, and from a very one-sided interpretation of other passages.

Throughout, the tone of M. Renan's criticism is of the same subjective character. Nothing weighs with him in comparison with his own internal judgment of the documents with which he deals. Tradition is of no account; Catholic opinion of no account; evidence, weighty in itself, because resting on facts which none can reasonably dispute, and therefore calculated equally to affect all minds, is nowhere urged by him—is apparently never even taken into consideration. While professing to base his inquiries on a historical, and not a theological foundation, he is yet dogmatic in the highest degree. The most subjective school of German theology is not more subjective or less soberly inductive than he is.

(2) M. Renan is, in truth, more than subjective in his criticism of the Gospels. He is arbitrary and personal in an unwonted measure. He not only separates himself from the Catholic interpretation of the Church, but he does not ally himself with any school of criticism. He is not careful to fortify his own judgments, even the most amazing of them, by the coincident opinions of scholars who have devoted their lives to the special studies upon which he has ventured in this volume. As a sceptic, he wages war with Catholic sentiment and tradition almost entirely at his own hand. To the great sceptical school of Germany, who have laboured with such perseverance

in this field, he scarcely alludes. He makes no use of their conclusions; he builds nothing upon them. And yet he professes that it is one of his principles not to do over again what has been well done.[1] He professes, in short, not once, but throughout, to work, as it were, from the centre of accumulated inquiries, historical and critical, which have all tended to the same result, and left many of the startling issues which he has popularized, beyond question in the eyes of all scholars. And yet he stands singularly aloof from any class of these inquiries, and pays no deference to them. For an orthodox critic[2] to write regarding

[1] Introduction, p. vi.

[2] This has been remarked by M. De Pressensé, who has written an excellent answer to M. Renan's volume—an answer which would have been still more excellent, if the writer had been here and there more intent upon the merits of his case and the satisfaction of his reader, than upon a personal triumph over M. Renan.

the Gospels, and to ignore the labours of the Tübingen divines, would be at once deemed a reproach to him—a mark of ignorance; but M. Renan apparently knows nothing of them, or at least makes no account of them. We do not blame him for this. But he is to be blamed for claiming everywhere a so-called *scientific* value for his conclusions,—which can only belong to them as the concurrent conclusions of many scholars, and as resting on indisputable data, to which historical criticism has at length given a consistent and irresistible meaning; and at the same time while claiming such an authority, we find him everywhere freely indulging in a spirit of the most arbitrary and unauthorized assertion. The truth is, that this pretence of scientific value for the views of an advanced sceptical criticism in this particular province of inquiry, is absurd. It has become a common-place of sceptical criticism, but has no better foundation than many other common-places which this criticism despises. For if there is one feature of the writings of this school more remarkable than another, it is what must be fairly called their utterly unscientific character—their confusion, mutual contradictions, and even contemptuous displacement of one another. As Strauss repudiates Paulus, so Renan repudiates Strauss. No book ever showed more plainly than the "Vie de Jésus" how unsettled this whole field of inquiry must be, regarded from a scientific-historical point of view. Whatever openings towards a scientific unanimity of opinion may be observable, are certainly not in the direction of M. Renan. Concord is least of all an attribute of sceptical historians and theologians. While heartily combining against Christianity, they show but little fraternal love and indulgence to each other's scepticisms. They level their lances against a common foe, but they also point them, often with equal ardour, against one another.

(3) But M. Renan's criticism is not only arbitrary and unauthorized; it is, moreover, inconsistent as an historical method. It stamps the Gospels, in so far as they are miraculous, with an inveterate incredibility, and yet it professes to use them as historical data for the life of Christ. The author even justifies this course by an appeal to the alleged parallels of the Lives of the Saints, and the necessity of a certain power of "divination and conjecture" in reproducing the great characters of the past. He claims the right, in short, and carries it into

practice everywhere thoughout his volume, to select and adapt the texts of the Gospels as he likes, accepting what suits him, and rejecting what does not fall in with his preconceptions and ideal. But this is not to write history. It is impossible to use documentary sources after such a fashion; or, at any rate, it is incompatible with any fair and consistent principles of historical criticism to do so. Legend and history must be kept in their respective places. The former may be a safe and valuable stimulant to the historical imagination, but it is useless —it may be often positively pernicious—as a guide to historical truth. And, particularly, a document cannot be regarded as at once legend and history, in the sense and to the degree, presumed by our author of the Gospels. The fallacy involved in his parallel of the Gospels to the Lives of the

Saints we shall afterwards see; but even if we were to grant this parallel, it would not serve M. Renan's purpose. For lives of Saints, as much filled with miracles, and therefore as legendary, as the Gospels are according to his view, would not be regarded by any school of historians, and least of all by the critical school to which he professes to belong, as historical documents, any more than the mythical narrative of Livy, or the heroic delineations of Homer. It would be a vain task, which no scholar would attempt, to reproduce the biographic lineaments of such saints, any more than of a mythical hero of the early ages of Greece and Rome. Ecclesiastical tradition and art-criticism may delight themselves with the imaginary characteristics and exploits of legendary saints, but such ideal portraits, religious or artistic, are recognised to belong to quite a different province from the historical. The Gospels, therefore, cannot be used in the double sense of M. Renan. The principles of that historical criticism to which he appeals are directly opposed to such an inconsistency. If they are legendary to the extent he supposes, they are worthless as historical documents. We cannot accept them with the one hand and reject them with the other; for they are homogeneous, if ever documents were—informed by one spirit, bearing one character, and stamped alike in their miraculous and their ordinary narrative by one consistent purpose and meaning.

IV.

Having explained the critical groundwork of the "Vie de Jésus," we now propose to examine this groundwork more carefully. We have remarked how personal, arbitrary, and unscientific it is, while making unusual scientific pretensions. The author does not rest his critical conclusions on full inquiry, and minute induction and argument. He is sentimental rather than judicial; highly authoritative, but the authority implying in the main little more than his own *ipse dixit*. The simple-minded reader—anxious to know the truth, and conscious of his ignorance of the Talmud, of Philo, and it may be even of Josephus —not to speak of the Zendevesta and the Boundehesch—is apt at first to be overwhelmed by the extraordinary confidence of the author; but the more carefully he reads, the less impression does this tone make upon him. And when he finds the same confidence and rashness of assertion carried into subjects of which he really knows something—for M. Renan loves to indulge his generalizing faculty and tendency to dogmatism on all subjects—he is able to estimate the book more according to its just proportions and value.

There are three points in M. Renan's critical account of the Gospels deserving attention. I. His view of the Gospels of St. Matthew and St. Mark. II. His estimate of the Fourth Gospel, and the supposed contradictions which it presents to that of Matthew. And, III. His general view of the Gospels as legendary biographies. We shall consider these several points in succession.

I. He proposes mainly to base his conclusions as to the Gospels of St. Matthew and St. Mark on an expression of Papias in a passage preserved by Eusebius. This passage implies, according to him, that the original Gospel of St. Matthew contained only the Logia, or discourses, which still form so large a part of it. St. Mark's Gospel, on the other hand, was originally little more than a collection of biographic anecdotes. It was only gradually, by a process which he describes, that these Gospels respectively assumed their present form. St. Matthew is "characterized by long discourses; St. Mark is above all anecdotical

—more exact than the first as to minute facts, brief even to dryness, poor in discourse, ill composed."

Now, whether this be a true account of these Gospels or not, it does not really correspond to the statement of Papias. There is no such marked contrast implied in his language as is here drawn from it. It is true Papias uses the expression *Λόγια*, and nothing else, in speaking of St. Matthew's Gospel; but the Gospel of St. Mark is described as containing *τὰ ὑπὸ τοῦ Χριστοῦ ἢ λεχθέντα ἢ πραχθέντα.*[1] Whatever, there-

[1] The following is the passage in full:—

Μάρκος μὲν ἑρμηνευτὴς Πέτρου γενόμενος, ὅσα ἐμνημόνευσεν, ἀκριβῶς ἔγραψεν. οὐ μέντοι τάξει τὰ ὑπὸ τοῦ Χριστοῦ ἢ λεχθέντα ἢ πραχθέντα. οὔτε γὰρ ἤκουσε τοῦ Κυρίου, οὔτε παρηκολούθησεν αὐτῷ. ὕστερον δὲ ὡς ἔφην Πέτρῳ, ὃς πρὸς τὰς χρείας ἐποιεῖτο τὰς διδασκαλίας. ἀλλ' οὐχ ὥσπερ σύνταξιν τῶν Κυριακῶν ποιούμενος λόγων. ὥς τε οὐ δὲν ἥμαρτεν Μάρκος, οὕτως ἔνια γράψας ὡς ἀπεμνημόνευσεν. ἑνὸς γὰρ ἐποιήσατο πρόνοιαν, τοῦ μηδὲν, ὧν ἤκουσεν, παραλιπεῖν, ἢ ψεύσασθαί τι

fore, may be the precise interpretation of *logia*, there is no warrant, so far as Papias is concerned, for the presumption that the Gospel of St. Mark was originally nothing more than a brief narrative of facts, or collection of anecdotes. It is expressly said to have contained the things "spoken" as well as "done" by our Lord. It would be impossible to use any expressions more fitly answering to the Gospel in its present form.

Is there really any more reason for supposing St. Matthew's Gospel to have been originally nothing more than a collection of discourses? The expression "Λόγια," no doubt, mainly suggests the idea of dis-

ἐν αὐτοῖς. ταῦτα μὲν οὖν ἱστόρηται τῷ Παπίᾳ περὶ τοῦ Μάρκου. περὶ δὲ τοῦ Ματθαίου ταῦτα εἴρηται, Ματθαῖος μὲν οὖν ἑβραιδ-διαλέκτῳ τὰ λόγια συνεγράψατο. ἡρμήνευσε δ' αὐτὰ ὡς ἠδύνατο ἕκαστος.—Euseb. H. E. iii. 39.

courses, or rather "oracles," but it may be held to bear the general historic sense of "annals;" it is maintained by competent and impartial critics that it must have this meaning here. According to a German critic,[1] who has made a special study of all the Patristic passages regarding the Gospels, in the interest of no school, it cannot have any other meaning, when viewed in

[1] Kirchhofer, in his Quellensammlung zur Geschichte d. Neut. Canons, p. 33. Lücke also maintains that the expression *τὰ λόγια* entirely corresponds to the parallel phrase applied to St. Mark's Gospel, *τὰ ὑπὸ τοῦ Χριστοῦ ἢ λεχθέντα ἢ πραχθέντα*—denoting as *denominatio a potiori* a writing embracing the relation of acts as well as discourses,—in the same manner as Papias, when he describes the Gospel of St. Mark, in the same passage, as *σύνταξις τῶν Κυριακῶν λόγων* does not mean to contradict his previous statement as to this Gospel containing *τὰ πραχθέντα* as well as *τὰ λεχθέντα*. This further phrase of Papias, indeed, would serve conclusively to settle the matter in the eyes of all who simply wish to ascertain his meaning, without having any theory to support.

its whole connexion, than that of an "account of our Lord's deeds as well as His discourses." It is absurd, therefore, to base a theory on this mere expression.

Further it deserves to be noticed that while M. Renan makes use for his own purpose of the words of Papias preserved by Eusebius, he entirely ignores another very distinct passage of Eusebius, where we are told that Matthew, "having in the first instance delivered his Gospel to his countrymen in their own language, afterwards, when he was about to leave them and extend his apostolic mission elsewhere, filled up, or completed his written Gospel, for the use of those whom he was leaving behind, as compensation for his absence."[1] This would

[1] Ματθαῖος μὲν γὰρ πρότερον Ἑβραίοις κηρύξας, ὡς ἔμελλε καὶ ἐφ' ἑτέρους ἰέναι, πατρίῳ γλώττῃ γραφῇ παραδοὺς τὸ κατ' αὐτὸν εὐαγγέλιον, τὸ λεῖπον τῇ αὐτοῦ παρουσίᾳ, τούτοις, ἀφ'

indicate that, whatever may have been the original character of St. Matthew's Gospel, it was afterwards supplemented, revised, and completed by himself.

Catholic tradition, and the voice of the Fathers, so far as it has been preserved,—of Irenæus,[1] Origen,[2] and Eusebius,[3]—unanimously presume the integrity of St. Matthew's Gospel from the beginning. Patristic authority, it is well known, is almost unanimous in asserting a Hebrew original of this Gospel, prepared by the Apostle specially for the use of his countrymen, and it is

ὧν ἐστέλλετο διὰ τῆς γραφῆς ἀπεπλήρου.—Euseb. Hist. Eccl. iii. 24. The phrase, τὸ λεῖπον τῇ αὐτοῦ παρουσίᾳ presents some ambiguity. Nicephorus has τὸ λεῖπον τῆς αὐτοῦ παρουσίας—*defectum præsentiæ suæ iis quos relinquebat, scripto compensavit*—a translation which we have virtually followed.

[1] Adv. Hær. iii. 1.

[2] Comm. in Matt. in Euseb. H. E. vi. 25.

[3] H. E. as above.

most unlikely that such a document would not contain a narrative of our Lord's miracles, as well as of His discourses. And when we turn to the Gospel itself, it is found to bear every appearance of undivided authorship. It is stamped throughout by a dominant impression,—a special and individual aim,—exactly answering to the Patristic idea of it. It is the *Gospel to the Hebrews*. The author is a Jew among Jews, and obviously writing for Jews. The great purpose of his Gospel, accordingly, is to exhibit Jesus as the Messiah—as the accomplishment of Hebrew prophecy—the fulfilment of the Law and the Prophets. Whatever Jesus may have been besides, He was also and primarily the Messiah, the highest development of Judaism, humanly speaking. He was not merely this accomplishment in an external sense, but the highest expression of all that was good in Judaism—the inheritor of whatever moral wisdom, whatever spiritual genius survived in it. Although we cannot, therefore, say with M. Renan—for it is neither consistent with reason nor evidence to say it, that Jesus Christ was "a disciple of Hillel,"—that He borrowed from the Jewish schools those charming moral utterances which Matthew has above all preserved in his Gospel—and that "Philo was his elder brother;" although we desiderate all historical authority for such statements, we do not doubt that Jesus Christ was wise according to all the wisdom of the Jews of His time. Whatever was beautiful, or touching, or sublime in the moral maxims of His country, shone with a yet higher beauty, pathos, and sublimity in His large intelligence, and came forth from Him in more living and perfect form than it had yet known. In this sense Jesus was a Rabbi among rabbis; the religious spirit of the old Dispensation culminated in Him. He was both its subjective and objective fulfilment; in whom at once its genius was consummated, and its historical function done away. And this Jesus, at once the greatest among Jews, and the finisher of Judaism—the Messiah—is the Jesus represented to us by St. Matthew. This is the image which the Gospel, not merely in parts, but as a whole, not in its discourses merely, but in its narrative also, constantly brings before us. This personality lives throughout its pages, binding them into a unity, animating them as a whole. And it is impossible that such a consistent picture could have been the result if the Gospel had been, as supposed, a mere mass of gradually accumulating tradition.

The evidence for the unity of the Gospel

of St. Mark as it now stands, is, if possible, still more conclusive. According to uniform Patristic tradition,[1] the force of which we confess impresses us the more we study it, this Gospel especially represents the teaching of St. Peter, of whom St. Mark was "companion," "disciple," "interpreter." The Gospel, in its very marked characteristics, exactly answers to this idea. Its picturesque brevity of style; the beautiful, affectionate hints that drop out here and there as to the looks, and manner, and attitude of our Lord; the simplicity and minuteness of its descriptive touches—as when it notes the colour of the grass on which the multitudes at the miraculous

[1] Papias in Euseb. H. E. iii. 39. Clemens Alex. in Euseb. H. E. ii. 25. Tertullian Adv. Marcion. ii. 5. Iren. Adv. Hær. iii. 10. Euseb. H. E. v. 8, vi. 14. Jerome Cat. Script. Eccl. c. 8; Ep. ad Hedib. c. 2.

feast sat down,[1] — the very curtness and inexpansiveness of its discourses, which M. Renan makes a reproach to it; all indicate the warm, impulsive, frank-hearted disciple, whose affections opened so keenly towards the Lord, and embraced so readily His higher character, but whose intelligence and strength of will obviously did not always keep pace with his affections; whose faculty of discourse, as his epistles and sermons in the Acts of the Apostles show, was not equal to his faculty of practical work and organization.

II. Our author's view of the fourth Gospel, is founded upon his inability to conceive the Son of Zebedee to be the writer of the long metaphysical discourses which characterize it. St. John according to him probably left notes behind him, but the

[1] Chap. vi. 39.

speculative elaboration and polemical turn of these notes must be attributed to his scholars at Ephesus, of whose character and history we know so little. One thing alone is certain with him, that this Gospel cannot be accepted as conveying a true picture of our Lord. M. Renan reiterates his confidence on this point, and suggests the theory of a double origin as the most likely explanation of the double character he finds in it; viz. its direct traces of originality on the one hand, and on the other its dogmatic reflective tone, so alien, in his estimation, from the spirit of Jesus Christ and his first disciples. It is sufficient to say in answer to all this, that the double character which M. Renan attributes to the fourth Gospel, is, like many other things in his volume, merely the creation of his own critical fancy. To other minds, and according to the almost uniform testimony of Biblical scholars, there is nothing inconsistent in the evident originality of the narrative of the fourth Gospel —which gives to it such a special historical value—and its prevailing dogmatic tone. The whole Gospel, with the exception perhaps of the twenty-first chapter, and two isolated portions[1] which have always been regarded as of doubtful authenticity, is plainly the production of one mind. The same spirit and style everywhere pervade its didactic and narrative parts. These cannot be separated and attributed to diverse authorship on any fair principle of literary interpretation. So far as it is possible to make sure of the unity of any composition by the identity of its spirit and structure throughout—and criticism always acknowledges the force of this evidence—it

[1] Chap. vi. 53; viii. 1—12.

is possible to certify the unity which marks the successive chapters of the fourth Gospel with almost a monotone of sentiment and of language. Here, as elsewhere, we may well set the judgment of Catholic scholarship against mere arbitrary opinionativeness. The majority even of sceptical theologians have united in affirming the unity of the fourth Gospel. They may deny its Apostolic authorship, but they acknowledge the irresistible evidence furnished by the Gospel itself of its having proceeded from a single mind of very marked individuality.

But what have we to say to the diversity between this Gospel and the synoptical Gospels, especially that of St. Matthew, so sharply drawn out by M. Renan? The two Gospels are not merely diverse in his view, but they are conflicting; the one excludes the other. Either St. Matthew must be wrong, or St. John must be wrong, he says, in the picture which they convey of our Lord, and the report of the discourses which they put into His mouth. The discourses of St. John, we are told, have nothing in common with the *logia* of St. Matthew in tone, style, or doctrine. If Jesus spoke as represented by the latter, He cannot have spoken as represented by the former. And between the two authorities, from our author's estimate, no critic can or will hesitate. He will recognise the Jesus of the first Gospel as the true Jesus, and the charming sentences which fell from Him on the Mount, and on the banks of the Lake of Gennesareth, as His genuine utterances.

Now the contrast between the first and fourth Gospel, or between the latter and the synoptics generally, has been always recognised. It has been a subject of devout study in the Church from the days of Clemens Alexandrinus. Both Clemens, and Origen after him, give a definite, and, in some respects, beautiful explanation of the difference.[1]

[1] Clemens, in a passage cited by Eusebius (H. E. vi. 14), descriptive of the origin of the Gospels generally, says: "that when John saw in the other Gospels outward or corporeal matters (τὰ σωματικὰ), he composed a spiritual Gospel (πνευματίκον ποιῆσαι εὐαγγέλιον)." The statement of Origen (Com. in Johan.) is more to the point: τολμητέον τοίνουν εἰπεῖν ἀπαρχὴν μὲν πασῶν γραφῶν εἶναι τὰ εὐαγγέλια, τῶν δὲ εὐαγγελίων ἀπαρχὴν τὸ κατὰ Ἰωάννην, οὗ τὸν νοῦν οὐδεὶς δύναται λαβεῖν μὴ ἀναπεσὼν ἐπὶ τὸ στῆθος Ἰησοῦ, μηδὲ λαβὼν ἀπὸ Ἰησοῦ τὴν Μαρίαν γινομένην καὶ αὐτοῦ μήτερα. "We may venture then to say that the first-fruit of all the Scriptures is the Gospels, and of the Gospels the first-fruit is that according to St. John, whose meaning no one can grasp unless he have leant on Jesus' bosom, or have received from Jesus, Mary, and she become his own mother."

In referring to these explanations, we do not mean to imply any opinion as to their accuracy or value. Whether we think them to the point or not, both passages are interesting in themselves, and serve very fitly to show the ancient interest of the Church in the peculiar character of St. John's Gospel.—We may take this opportunity of stating that it has been our aim throughout the text to keep clear of any questions as to the

Eusebius,[1] also, from a separate point of view, endeavours to explain it. The sub-

Gospels, save those which M. Renan forces upon us. We could not otherwise have kept to our special task, or accomplished it within any due limits—so many points arise on all sides for discussion as to the relative origin and character of the Gospels. Scarcely any province of critical inquiry presents more conflicting theories. Those who deny the supplementary theory of the origin of St. John's Gospel—concluding that the Apostle had never seen any of the other Gospels—pay little deference of course to such statements as those of Clemens and Origen. It appears to us, however, that it is impossible to disregard these statements altogether, especially while resting so confidently as we do on the testimony of the same Fathers to the genuineness of the Gospels. We regret, therefore, to notice that, in the last edition of his Greek Testament, Dean Alford goes the length of repudiating a Hebrew original of St. Matthew's Gospel, in the face of evidence which, with all possible deductions, seems irresistible; and that he is even disposed to treat slightly the unvarying Patristic traditions as to the connexion of St. Peter with the Gospel of St. Mark. If the testimony of the Fathers is good for anything at all, this connexion is as certain as any historical fact can be, and not less important than it is certain.

[1] H. E. iii. 24.

ject is one which Christian scholars have never shrunk from discussing, and which yields, when fairly and fully examined, a testimony to the exalted character of the doctrine of Christ, rather than an embarrassment in the reception of it.

There is, indeed, a striking difference between the first and the fourth Gospels, but there is no contradiction. Between the Sermon on the Mount, and such arguments as fill the sixth chapter of the Gospel of St. John, and the touching discourses of our Lord in the latter chapters of the same Gospel, there is a wide distinction, but there is no discrepancy. St. John represents a special side of our Lord's Divine character and doctrine which St. Matthew has only slightly touched. Whatever view we take of the origin of the fourth Gospel, it was obviously written in circumstances wholly different from those in which St. Matthew composed his Gospel. New tendencies had sprung up in the Church, new forms of error had begun to shew themselves. The Christian consciousness had developed and matured, and was able both to enter more fully into the mind of Christ, and to recall more fully the expression of that mind given in the days of His flesh. The Spirit was accomplishing His promised mission to "guide" the apostolic mind "into all truth." And so from the lessons of this higher and more mature consciousness of what Christ was, and of many things that He spake, arose the fourth Gospel—very distinct in character from the others, bringing into clearer view certain specially divine aspects of Christ's doctrine, but nowhere opposing the teaching of the synoptics; unfolding and explaining that teaching, but in no respect contradicting it. M. Renan, notwithstanding all he says on the subject, does not venture to point out any contradictions. The truth is, that the Gospel of St. John and the other Gospels are too much apart to contradict each other. Their very diversity saves them from opposition. Their mode of composition, their purpose, their style are distinct. The synoptics are in the main merely historical and descriptive. St. John is dogmatic as well as historical. He has evidently the conscious purpose throughout of representing our Lord in His more divine relations; as He appeared not merely to the more limited Jewish apprehension, but to the fully informed and comprehensive Christian conception (*gnosis*).

And there is nothing surprising in the fact that so manifold and sublime a Personality as our Lord's should thus appear to different minds so different, or that His teaching should be capable of being exhibited with equal truth in two such diverse forms. Even granting Jesus to have only been such a character as M. Renan allows Him to have been—a man in whom the consciousness of the Divine rose to a pitch of unexampled exaltation—there is really nothing unlikely in this. Rather it is extremely likely that such a character in such circumstances should appear in one case mainly as the Galilean Prophet and Teacher of a Divine morality; in the other as a Divine Thinker and Doctor in the highest sense. Granting for a moment the justice of the picture, fanciful as it really is, which describes him as a beautiful Galilean youth, inspired by a radiant spiritual intelligence, seeking vent in the most exquisite ethical aphorisms,—is it at all strange that the same youth should become a Teacher of the highest spiritual philosophy, dogmatic or polemical, as suited His subject and audience? Surely not. M. Renan allows that the ideas of Jesus underwent a change as He advanced in His career; that He became less simple, less expository, more vehement, more denunciatory. Is it more inconsistent with real unity of character that He should at one time have been more the mere Preacher on the Mount, at another time more the lofty Theologian, at another time the meditative Thinker, revelling in the consciousness of His supreme relation with the Father, and from the height of that supreme communion, making known its mysteries to His assembled disciples, before they should be separated from His earthly presence? M. Renan cannot conceive the moral aphorisms of St. Matthew and the metaphysics of St. John to proceed from the same mind. But may not this be as much owing to his own narrowness of conception, as to anything inconceivable in the combination itself? On the contrary, it has appeared to the Church, and to Biblical scholars in general, that there is not only nothing unintelligible in such a combination, but that in truth the wonder would have been if so sublime a Personality had not been presented to us in two such diverse but nowhere contradictory lights.

But we must further maintain, that not only is there no contradiction in the testimony of the two Evangelists, but that a genuine criticism is everywhere able to elicit a clear harmony and even identity in their views. Their representations are not commensurate, but they touch and unite at different points. The Jesus of St. John claims more uniformly a Divine dignity, surrounds Himself more obviously with a Divine light, making Himself equal with the Father in power and glory; but no less does the Jesus of St. Matthew claim and accept Divine homage, and exercise Divine prerogatives. He forgives sins;[1] He accepts worship;[2] He elicits from St. Peter the declaration that He is the Son of God[3]—no mere prophet or teacher, but the Son of God in a sense in which no prophet was before Him. In a well-known passage,[4] He declares that "all things are delivered to Him of the Father; and no man knoweth the Son but the Father; neither knoweth any man the Father save the Son, and he to whomsoever the Son will reveal Him." Such statements

[1] Matt. ix. 2. [2] xiv. 33.
[3] xvi. 15, 16. [4] xi. 27.

breathe the very spirit which pervades St. John; they are comparatively isolated, but they are there, clear and emphatic. It is impossible to empty such statements of dogmatic import and not to recognise that they are meant to carry on the mind, as it were, from the mere idea of a Galilean Teacher to that of a Divine Person—from the Sermon on the Mount to the prologue of the fourth Gospel. This is surely the natural view of the question, even as a mere literary question. Two documents survive which profess to represent the public career of one who, by His spiritual greatness, has influenced the world more than any other person who ever lived. One of these documents represents His teaching in its more simple elements—in its popular moral relations, so to speak; the other represents His teaching in its higher meanings—its more theological relations. The teaching in the one case does not contradict that in the other; it only supplements and crowns it. In its simpler elements, as contained in the earlier document, there is not the same uniform assertion of the higher theological truth, but there are everywhere the indications of it, pointing the mind forward to that higher truth. Is not this fact what we might expect? and does not the recognition of Jesus as at once the Messiah and the Son of God—as at once the Son of Man and equal with the Father—harmonise with the literary facts and explain them; while no other supposition does this, but leaves both the facts unexplained, and the personality or character unsolved?

III. But there is still a further point in M. Renan's critical estimate of the Gospels that claims special notice. The right view of the Gospels, he tells us, is that of legendary biographies. The image of St. Francis of Assisi constantly occurs to him as a historical phenomenon similar to our Lord; and the biographies of the saint, and others, are suggested as parallels to the Gospels. This is one of the most extraordinary statements, we venture to say, that has ever been made even in the literature of unbelief, and the very piquancy of its dogmatism is apt to impose upon the popular reader. It excites his imagination; it takes even his intellect by surprise. What a natural idea! he is apt to think. His mind feels a species of satisfaction in being furnished with such a novel explanation of the Gospels. They form no longer an exceptionable, unaccountable literature; they take their place as ordinary phenomena in literary history. The mythical theory has been proved to be unsatisfactory. It throws the whole task of the creation of the Gospel upon the Messianic imagination of the first Disciples — an utterly inadequate cause. According to our author, the disciples were incapable of comprehending the Divine original presented to them. So far as they could, they have marred the picture rather than made it. The personality of Jesus was a reality, just as that of St. Francis was, but the records of His life have become mixed with fabulous traditions, like those of the mediæval saint. This was only inevitable. Jesus would not only have been an extraordinary, but a wholly unexampled character, if such legendary matter had not gathered around his life. The life of Alexander had already become inextricably mixed up with legend before the death of his companions in arms. The legend of St. Francis had begun before his own death.

But there is a simple answer to all this pleasant inventiveness. There is really no literary parallel between the Gospels and the lives of the saints. Save in so far as both present a combination of miraculous and ordinary incident, they are in every respect different. The lives of the saints are of two classes; sometimes—as in the lives of the patron saint of England, and of the four great virgin-martyrs of the Roman Catholic Church—the matter is entirely legendary, and mostly miraculous; in other cases—as in that of the lives of St. Francis of Assisi, and even more characteristically, perhaps, of St. Bernard — the legendary-miraculous element is distinct, and capable of being separated from the intelligible outline of undeniable facts and features composing the real lives of these hero-saints. Nay, it may be said that, in almost every case, the addition of the legendary-miraculous matter can be traced as an after-growth—the real life of the saint standing clear apart from it, and being found described without miraculous admixture in some earlier record. For example, of the very St. Francis to whom M. Renan so often refers, we possess three lives, two of them written by contemporaries,[1] and one of them—the most famous—by Bonaventura, in the generation immediately following. The process of miraculous addition to the incidents of St. Francis' life can be plainly noted in these almost coeval biographies. Thomas of Celano, his first biographer, ascribes to him no wonders

[1] Thomas de Celano, and the "Tres Socii," or three associates of the saint.

except the cure of sickness. The natural features of the saint appear sufficiently marvellous, yet sufficiently intelligible. But gradually miraculous accretions gather round his life. In the biography by Bonaventura, it is recorded that the intercession of the saint was successful in restoring sight to a blind man. This would be almost contemporary testimony. But the Bollandist editors have discovered that the passage containing this alleged miracle was not the production of Bonaventura himself, but was inserted in the work after his death. Thus we see the formation of the legendary miraculous matter in the life of St. Francis, and at the same time see the life standing quite apart from it. And the very same thing is true of St. Francis' great contemporary—St. Dominic. His later biographies are crowded with miracles; but his first biographer declares that the miraculous stories he had heard were so conflicting, that he did not venture to record them.

It is to the latter class of the lives of the saints, of course, that M. Renan refers, in drawing a comparison between them and the Gospels. But who does not, even in our brief statement, recognise the broad distinction between the two? St. Francis, St. Bernard, or St. Dominic are not only intelligible, but they are distinctly-marked historical characters, quite apart from any of the legendary miracles attributed to them. There are lives of them extant in which the miraculous element holds no place, or, at least, a place so unimportant and accidental that it may be dropped out, and the narrative be all the more consistent and intelligible. But in the Gospels, the miracle is not merely a part of the narrative, it is the main narrative. The miraculous elements of our Lord's life are the characteristic elements; His life is a supernatural life throughout, and so the Gospels begin with miracles and end with miracles. The supernatural is the cohesive thread of the narrative, and if dropped out, the life itself would disappear. M. Renan does not dare to class the Gospels with such mere fables as the traditionary lives of St. George, or St. Christopher, or St. Ursula, or St. Catherine; and yet the life of our Lord would be almost as blank as the lives of these saints, with the miraculous elements withdrawn from it. The parallel suggested by him, therefore, is utterly inapplicable. The legendary biographies of the saints form a literature which, if not without its puzzles to the historical student, is yet sufficiently intelligible. It sprang up in an atmosphere of legend and of miraculous exaggeration. The beliefs to which it appealed were ready made, and so importunate as to demand material to feed upon. There is nothing analogous in the character or origin of the Gospels. The supernatural life which they picture was not a life in harmony with predominant Jewish interests or even prevailing Jewish beliefs and sympathies. Unlike the mediæval miracles, the miracles of the Gospels were not wrought in support of a powerful Church or sect. They were wrought, on the contrary, in attestation of a mission repudiated and despised by the Jewish powers, Pharisee and Sadducee alike. All, in short, that serves to explain the legendary-miraculous literature of the middle ages is wanting in the case of the Evangelical miracles; and it is only an imagination such as M. Renan's that could possibly suppose the Gospels satisfactorily accounted for by being compared to the lives of the saints. A higher historical imagination—a more comprehensive critical intellect, looking merely at the literary facts —must at once reject such a comparison, as unfounded and unworthy.

V.

We have hitherto been employed in exposing the philosophical and critical assumptions which lie at the basis of M. Renan's book. We now approach the substance of the book itself, which we shall treat, as far as is necessary, in two lectures. Nor is there any disproportion in this mode of treatment, for the poison of the book really lies in those assumptions with which we have been dealing; and clearly to make them understood is to show in the best manner how unfounded the book is, and how absurd and untenable are its historical pretensions. For if the Christian is not warranted to set out from the assumption of the supernatural, still less surely can the sceptic be entitled to start from the assumption of its denial and impossibility. The Christian has, at least, the assenting tradition of Christendom—the common faith of humanity—on his side. What has the Positivist on his side?—The conclusions of a partial and polemical philosophy—conclusions of yesterday, which, if accepted by one or two distinguished men and a herd of imitators, have not won the assent of a single really great mind, in which the springs of faith lie deep beside the wells of science—at once acute and comprehensive, spiritual and logical. To send abroad to the world a "Life of Jesus" founded on the assumptions of such a philosophy, without a single word in vindication of them, argues a confidence quite as remarkable as the most absolute faith, on which the author looks with pity. Nor is the criticism of the volume more free from assumption than its philosophy—more weighty in itself, or better sustained. While claiming an eminently historical character, it has really no historical value. It is a mere abuse of language to term such criticism, scientific. To call the Gospels legendary narratives, like the lives of the mediæval saints, and to suppose, apart from all deeper questions, that they are thereby sufficiently explained as mere literary phenomena, implies a wonderful insensibility or a wonderful credulity.

But let us now turn to the Life which M. Renan presents us, and test his labours by their result. Is it a consistent intelligible Life which he has drawn? Does it harmonize with his conclusions and the admitted facts of the case? The aim of every biographer of Jesus must be to explain the marvellous Ideal which the Gospels bring before him. It is this ideal which fastens the gaze of scepticism as well as the eye of faith. It has confessedly fascinated and "charmed" our author; he gives voice to his admiration in many places, and cannot sufficiently utter the moral delight with which it fills him. How has he succeeded, then, in drawing this ideal on the principles from which he starts? Has it any *vraisemblance*, artistically, morally, or historically? Is it intelligible on any of the ordinary principles on which we interpret the great phenomena of history and of life? These are fair questions to ask; they touch the centre of all historical treatment of the Gospels; for who shall define the intimate association in every case between our view of the Gospels and of the Christ which they represent? The picture fits the frame, and the frame the picture. They shed a reflected glory on one another. It is the divine perfection of the ideal which more than all stamps a divine completeness and authority upon the several sources of its expression. This is the higher light which lightens every Christian intelligence, and around which all the phenomena of the Evangelical history fall into harmony and receive their explanation. What does M. Renan make of this ideal? How does his Life harmonize with his materials—with itself, with the known facts of history? We shall devote this lecture to explanation; in the next, we shall examine the picture set before us.

It is needless to say that M. Renan

ignores the alleged supernatural birth of our Lord. Here, as elsewhere, he calmly sets aside the testimony of the Gospels whenever it suits him. There was no such birth at Bethlehem as St. Luke describes. The notion of such a birth sprang from the later effort to connect Jesus with the lineage of David—a connexion which could have no historical foundation, for the race of David had long before passed away. He was born at Nazareth, and was known as a Nazarene all his life. He sprang from a family in the middle walks of life, not rich, yet not miserably poor—of the rank of artizans living by their labour. Our author has drawn a lively picture of the character of such a family in the East, and of the supposed circumstances in the midst of which Jesus spent his youth. External nature, a singularly beautiful and happy disposition, the floating moralisms and wide-spread, deeply-exciting Messianic dreams of His country—these are the influences which made Jesus what He was—the causes out of which Christianity sprang. All who have read M. Renan's volume will admit the fairness of this statement. His explanations nowhere go beyond these resources. He speaks, indeed, in his Introduction, of Philo, and calls him the elder brother of Jesus; he speaks of the "excellent maxims of the love of God, of charity, of rest in God," in the writings of the illustrious Alexandrian thinker,[1] which find their echo in the Gospel; but he does not attempt to connect Jesus with Philo, or to attribute any influence to the latter over the former. He admits, on the contrary—what, indeed, he could not help admitting

[1] P. 35.

—that Philo remained utterly unknown to Jesus, as Jesus probably did to Philo, although the latter survived the date of the crucifixion about twenty years. He speaks, also, of the Talmud, and in some places ascribes to it, or rather to the oral teaching out of which it grew (for the date of the Talmud, he confesses, cannot be higher than the year 200), a definite influence on the moral education of Jesus. "The true notion of the circumstances in which Jesus was produced must be sought," he says, "in this *bizarre* compilation, where the most precious truths are mixed with the most insignificant scholasticism." [1] But he rejoices, at the same time, that Jesus was happily beyond the circle of the Pharisaic scholasticism, which formed the germ of the Talmud. He does not, in short, at-

[1] Introd. xii.

tempt to connect Jesus with any school of thought or religious instruction. The Essenes, the Pharisees, the Sadducees, were alike unknown to Him during the period of His youthful education in Galilee. Possibly, the principles of Hillel, who fifty years before had delivered aphorisms very like His own, were not unknown to Him. He leaves this to be inferred. He even says, with his characteristic confidence, that Hillel was the true teacher of Jesus[1]—a statement for which there is not the slightest historical foundation.

What then is his explanation of Christianity? Virtually this: It sprang up out of the bosom of Jewish culture *in Galilee.* Jesus was a son of the Galilean soil, where, according to M. Renan, he was born and nurtured—nothing more. It is a glowing

[1] P. 35.

romance, dazzling with imaginary colours, that he draws. Let us look at it. Christianity, he says, could only have sprung out of this northern region of Palestine. Its natural splendours are all in harmony with the joyous spirit of the infancy of the Gospel.

"With a less brilliant development in one sense than Jerusalem, Galilee was yet far more fertile in real greatness; the most living works of the Jewish people had always come from it. Jerusalem, on the contrary, was characterized by a complete absence of the sentiment of nature; a spirit dry, narrow and stern, had left upon all its features an impress, sublime, but sad, arid and repulsive. With its solemn doctors, its insipid canonists, its atrabilious hypocrites, Jerusalem would never have conquered humanity. The North alone has given to the world the *naïve* Shulamite, the humble Canaanite, the penitent Magdalen, the good foster-father Joseph, the Virgin Mary—the North alone has made Christianity. Jerusalem, on the contrary, was the true home of the obstinate Judaism which, founded by the Pharisees, and fixed by the Talmud, has crossed the Middle Age and survived even to our own time. A ravishing nature contributed to form the less austere, less bitterly monotheistic spirit, so to speak, which gave a charming and idyllic impress to all the dreams of Galilee."[1]

The country around Jerusalem, he adds, is, perhaps, the saddest in the world, while the North is beautifully green, umbrageous and smiling; "the true country of the Canticles, of the Songs of the Beloved;" where flowers and fruits abound, and where

[1] P. 64.

"the voice of the turtle" and the "singing of birds" is heard[1]—a country of lilies, and fig-trees, and vines; where the wine is excellent, and where they drink a good deal of it.

[1] "La Galilée au contraire, était un pays très-vert, très-ombragé, très-souriant, le vrai pays du Cantique des Cantiques et des Chansons du Bien-Aimé. Pendant les deux mois de Mars et d'Avril, la campagne est un tapis de fleurs, d'une franchise de couleurs incomparable. Ses animaux y son petits, mais d'une douceur extrême. Des tourterelles sveltes et vives, des merles bleus si légers qu'ils posent sur une herbe sans la faire plier, des alouettes huppées, que viennent presque se mettre sous les pieds du voyageur, de petites tortues de ruisseaux, dont l'œil est vif et doux, des cigognes à l'air pudique et grave, dépouillant toute timidité, se laissent approcher de très-près par l'homme et semblent l'appeler. En aucun pays du monde, les montagnes ne se deploient avec plus d'harmonie et n'inspirent de plus hautes pensées. Jésus semble les avoir particulièrement aimées. Les actes les plus importants de sa carrière divine se passent sur les montagnes; c'est là qu'il était le mieux inspiré, c'est là qu'il avait avec les ancien prophètes de secrets entretiens, et qu'il se montrait aux yeux de ses disciples déjà transfiguré."—Pp. 64, 65.

It is astonishing with what elaborate delicacies of expression our author has wrought up his picture of Galilean scenery; a picture with charming touches here and there, but also somewhat marred by that over-done colouring and artificial neatness which so often palls in French art.

Such was the cradle of Christianity; and the whole history of the infant Gospel, in conformity with the character of its origin, was a "kind of delicious pastoral. A Messiah at marriage feasts, the harlot and the good Zaccheus invited to the banquet, the founders of the kingdom of heaven a procession of bridal nymphs—see what Galilee has attempted, and what it has caused to be accepted. Greece has traced charming *tableaux* of human life in sculpture and in poetry, but always without vanishing depths or distant horizons. Here are wanting marble—excellent artists—a language exquisite and refined: but withal, Galilee has created the sublimest ideal of the popular imagination; for the fate of humanity is transacted behind its idyll, and the light which illumines its *tableaux* is the Sun of the Kingdom of God."

So far as M. Renan's general descriptions can be resolved into clear and definite affirmations, the two main sources of the Evangelical doctrine, according to him, were the moral aphorisms of Judaism, and the Messianic ideas then everywhere prevalent.

The Sermon on the Mount was a happy adaptation of truths which were already familiar in the synagogue. They acquire a tone of emotion, and a certain poetry of authority in the mouth of Jesus; but this is all. The maxims themselves had been long in circulation.[1] Exquisite as is the form which Jesus gave them—and M. Renan allows to the Sermon on the Mount the utmost originality of form, it is "the highest creation which ever proceeded from the human conscience, the most beautiful code of the perfect life ever traced by moralist"—yet it possesses no originality of substance; it is capable of being entirely recomposed from ancient sources.[2]

In like manner the Messianic ideas, out of which Jesus wrought His conception of the "Kingdom of God," the "Kingdom of Heaven," were the common property of all Jews of the time. Originating with the older prophets, they had received a striking expression in the Book of Daniel and the Books of Enoch; the former of these writings especially, to which the great

[1] Pp. 81, 82. [2] P. 84.

crisis of the Maccabean struggle gave birth, had embodied these ideas in a more definite form than before, and impressed them widely upon the popular imagination. M. Renan has no doubt about the origin of the Book of Daniel. Beyond all question it belongs to the age of Antiochus Epiphanes, and takes no higher rank than the other apocryphal books. It is needless to say that the distinction of apocryphal and canonical has no existence for him.

These Messianic ideas were in his view essentially popular. "They were not taught in any school, but they were in the air," and the soul of Jesus was early penetrated by them. He yielded himself up entirely to them, undisturbed by any reflective care or sentimental anxiety. "Our temptations, our doubts never touched him. On the top of that Mount of Nazareth, where no modern man could sit without an unquiet, perhaps frivolous feeling as to his destiny, Jesus sat twenty times without a single doubt; free from egotism, the source of our sadness, and which makes us anxiously forecast the future, He thought only of His work, of His race, of humanity. Those mountains, that sea, that azure heaven, those lofty plains in the horizon, were for Him no melancholy vision of a soul which interrogates nature regarding its fate, but the sure symbol, the transparent shadow of an invisible world, and of a new heaven."[1]

According to M. Renan, then, our Lord was neither more nor less than the typical Galilean of His time. All the moral wisdom of the synagogue was found in Him, clothed in better and more beautiful forms; He wrought it into a more

[1] Pp. 55, 56.

exquisite creation of art than any teacher of the synagogue had yet done. All the passionate hopes of a higher kingdom and glory for Israel, which fermented in the popular Jewish imagination, were His in their utmost freedom and joyfulness of excitement. And to these two sources may be traced all that is characteristic in the matter of His teaching. So far he denies to Christ any originality; but he is too clear-sighted not to see that, notwithstanding his statements about the moral axioms of the synagogue, and the Messianic dreams of the people, and his elaborate praise of the glories of nature in Galilee, he is far from having explained the personality and career of Jesus. He is forced into the confession of the profound originality of Jesus after all. The growth of a powerful personality like His is not to be supposed subject to rigorous law. "A lofty notion of divinity, which He did not owe to Judaism, but which seems to have been entirely the creation of His own great soul, was, in some manner, the principle of all His strength." "He believed Himself to be in direct relation with God—He believed Himself to be the Son of God. The highest consciousness of God which has ever existed in the bosom of humanity has been that of Jesus."[1]

Such is the Christ of M. Renan's volume—a moral genius sprung from the decaying root of Judaism. All of divine life that survived in Judaism centred in Him; its moral precepts; its Messianic hopes; and, touched with the celestial fire of His great soul—kindled into new life by the breath of the divine consciousness that was in

[1] Pp. 73—75.

Him more than in any man before or since—they became Christianity. Çakya-Mouni, the founder of Buddhism; Plato, St. Paul, St. Francis of Assisi, St. Augustine, were all men of the same spirit. To them, too, has it been given to manifest the Divine in this world. But Jesus is before all: the Founder not merely of a new religion, but of the universal religion of humanity—the religion of the Spirit.

This, at least, was the primary aim of Jesus, the essential idea of His work. But, like all other reformers, Jesus was unable to carry out His original aim in its purity, and by the merely moral means which He Himself desired. He could not escape the superstitious excitements and wild desires of His time, which lived in the supernatural, and constantly craved for its supposed manifestations. The first conception which Jesus entertained of the kingdom of God, was a purely moral conception. "The kingdom of God is within you," He said to those who were restlessly seeking for external signs of its approach. "The Jesus who has founded the true kingdom of God—the kingdom of the sweet and of the humble —behold, the Jesus of the first time, pure and unmixed, when the voice of His Father resounded in His bosom with perfect harmony."[1]

But, ere long, we see a change, if not in His character, yet in His mode of action. This alleged change M. Renan is pleased to connect with John the Baptist. There is no part of his volume in which he has manifested a more arbitrary spirit than in his descriptions of the Baptist, and

[1] P. 80.

the relation which he held to Jesus. According to him, John was no forerunner of Christ, but rather a rival leader and teacher, possessing an earlier authority, which would probably have produced difficulties, had not his arrest and death withdrawn him from the scene. As it was, it appears to have been during His intercourse with the Baptist, that the views of Jesus regarding the kingdom of God underwent a change. His preaching henceforth became more formal and authoritative. His watchword was henceforth the announcement of the near approach of the divine kingdom. He was no longer merely a delightful moralist, aspiring to embody in lively and brief aphorisms sublime lessons; He became a transcendent revolutionist, who tries to renew the world from its foundation, and to establish upon earth the ideal which He has conceived.[1] Thus the moral gradually vanished in the millenial conception of the kingdom of God. This world is full of evil, Satan is its king; the good are persecuted and oppressed. Priests and doctors impose on others what they do not themselves perform. But God will yet arise and revenge His "saints." And the day of recompense is at hand. It will come suddenly, as "a thief in the night." The present world will be overturned, and all that is great in it laid low, and all that is weak in it exalted. "The first shall be last, and the last first." Now the good and evil are mixed together, like the wheat and tares in a field of grain; but the hour of their separation approaches, when each shall receive their definite and everlasting fate. And who is to accomplish this great

[1] P. 116, chap. vii.

change? Who is to establish the new kingdom? Jesus Himself. He is the universal Reformer; and it is by Him and His doings that God is to reign upon the earth. All the powers of nature are subject to Him for that purpose, and He believes that He can move them at His will.[1]

The contradiction thus apparent between the moral and millenarian doctrines of Christ, is strangely represented as the cause of His highest triumph. "It was just this contradiction which caused the success of His work. The millenarian by himself would have accomplished nothing durable: the moralist by himself would have accomplished nothing powerful. Millenarianism gave the immediate impulse: the moral doctrine secured the future. And thus Christianity united in itself two conditions

[1] Chap. vii. *passim.*

of its greatest success—a point of revolutionary departure, and the possibility of life."[1]

So in a similar manner Jesus became a worker of miracles—a thaumaturgist. According to our author the miracles of Jesus were an after-thought—an expedient to which He was driven to have recourse, or else abandon His mission. For miracles were then deemed the indispensable mark of divine claims. It was understood that the Messiah would perform many. "Jesus then had no alternative but to renounce His mission, or become a thaumaturgist."[2] He knew nothing besides, as we have already seen, of the higher philosophy of the Greek schools; He had no conception of "general laws," and an inviolable order of nature. He believed that human power could influence

[1] Chap. vii. [2] P. 257.

natural events; and the idea of miracles, therefore, excited in Him no surprise. Yet we are led to suppose that the working of miracles were something uncongenial to the better nature of Jesus. He became a thaumaturgist *à contre-cœur*, against His will, and continually manifested impatience under the necessities which it imposed upon Him.

All that concerns this subject is deeply painful in M. Renan's book. It could not but be so. His principles bound him to repudiate all supernatural pretension. A miracle in his eyes could be only a delusion or imposture. It is impossible, with any regard to the statements of the Gospels (allowing ever so much for their alleged legendary intermixtures), to deny that Jesus did profess to work miracles. M. Renan would fain evade the conclusion;

but he cannot. It is forced upon him; and in a single memorable case, the raising of Lazarus, he attempts to grapple with it. Never was there a more hopeless task; and the higher feeling and reason of M. Renan himself must blush when he reperuses that miserable scene around the tomb of Lazarus, which he has drawn in his twenty-first chapter. We do not venture to lift the veil upon it. We will only say that, were there nothing else to prove the absurdity of the ideal which he attempts to fix through all his pages, this scene were enough to destroy that ideal for ever. The most "vulgar rationalism" never imposed a baser interpretation on any biblical incident. The scepticism of the "Age of Reason" never drew a more unworthy picture.[1]

1 "La famille de Béthanie put être amenée presque sans s'en douter à l'acte important qu'on désirait. Jésus y

We are told, indeed, how great and good men in every agé have been the subject of errors—how Columbus was a dreamer, and

était adoré. Il semble que Lazare était malade, et que ce fut même sur un message des sœurs alarmées que Jésus quitta la Pérée. La joie de son arrivée put ramener Lazare à la vie. Peut-être aussi l'ardent désir de fermer la bouche à ceux qui niaient outrageusement la mission divine de leur ami entraîna-t-elle ces personnes passionnées au-delà de toutes les bornes. Peut-être Lazare, pâle encore de sa maladie, se fit-il entourer de bandelettes comme un mort et en fermer dans son tombeau de famille. Ces tombeaux étaient de grandes chambres taillées dans le roc, où l'on pénétrait par une ouverture carrée, que fermait une dalle énorme. Marthe et Marie vinrent au-devant de Jésus, et, sans le laisser entrer dans Béthanie, le conduisirent à la grotte. L'émotion qu'éprouva Jésus près du tombeau de son ami, qu'il croyait mort, put être prise par les assistants pour ce trouble, ce frémissement qui accompagnaient les miracles ; l'opinion populaire voulant que la vertu divine fût dans l'homme comme un principe épileptique et convulsif. Jésus (toujours dans l'hypothèse ci-dessus énoncée) désira voir encore une fois celui qu'il avait aimé, et, la pierre ayant été écartée, Lazare sortit avec ses bandelettes et la tête entourée d'un suaire."—P. 361.

how Newton believed in his own foolish explanations of the Apocalypse—how the great men of the Middle Ages, how Joan of Arc, came near to deception in many of their most illustrious acts. But the moral, nay, the historical reason refuses to take any satisfaction from such parallels; its wounds cannot be healed by such anodynes. Could we allow for a moment the validity of such a criticism of the Gospel history, all divine light and beauty must vanish from its pages. The fane that has been kept sacred in our hearts would be desecrated; the ideal which has been bright to us when all else was dark, would lie shivered and soiled—our hopes shaken with it—and our souls darkened, with no dawn to break on them any more.

It is unnecessary to prolong this sketch. The sort of 'Life' which M. Renan has attempted is sufficiently apparent. We are not conscious in any respect of misrepresenting him. We have allowed him, as far as possible, to speak in his own words; words, it must be granted, which in their polished precision never fail to convey his meaning, if they yet often, in their very delicacy and luxuriant neatness, seem to jar with the deeper interests and graver bearings of his subject.

It must further be allowed, that there are aspects of the subject which his scholarly penetration and historic liveliness serve to bring into fuller and more vivid light than before. No one has more clearly apprehended the material circumstances, and in some respects, the external characteristics, in the midst of which Christianity arose. The local features of Palestine; the state of the Jewish people and their rulers; the factions of Pharisee and Sadducee; the proud godless intolerance of the priesthood, and especially of the powerful family represented by Annas and Caiaphas, that held the chief power in their hands; the relation of these factions to the Roman authorities; the characters of Pilate and of Herod; all stand depicted in his pages in very graphic, interesting, and intelligible outline. And the manner in which he has contrived to bring forward these accessory realities in the life of Jesus, has given, in parts, a peculiar air of fact to his Life, and especially to the narrative of its closing scenes. The pathos of those scenes, so utterly beyond the dream of fiction, lives fresh and tender beneath all the unbelief of the philosopher and all the negations of the critic. The artist is more natural, less artificial, in the face of their tremendous reality; and the Christian student may gather profit, if he must also get pain, from their perusal. The success with which M. Renan has handled these accessories of his subject, particularly the portraits of Annas and of Pilate, only serves to bring into more prominent relief his utter failure in regard to his main subject. The human aspects of his story are quite within his reach, and come from his pen in lively and impressive colours: but the Divine life transcends his conception; and, misinterpreted alike in its origin and meaning, comes forth from his pages, as we shall show, an inconsistent, unintelligible, and distorted picture.

VI.

It remains for us to consider more closely the portrait drawn by M. Renan, and to test the value of his work by its effect. This is especially the test which his work invites—which the subject invites. For it must be the special aim of every biographer of Jesus to explain as far as he can the historical conditions under which He arose; the combination of influences by which His character was moulded, and which constituted His unexampled individuality. We have seen how M. Renan tries to do this. Let us examine the result.

In whatever degree it is fair to judge of ordinary biography by its result, by the *vraisemblance* of the portrait presented, it must be fair to apply such a test to a biography of Jesus, and to judge of its success accordingly. For of all characters, His is the most prominent, the most marked and impressive that the world has ever seen. By universal consent, no such personality has ever before or since existed. M. Renan fully and frankly admits this—that among men, Jesus of Nazareth is without peer; the greatest in Himself, the greatest in the impulse which He has communicated to the world. There is no religion whose interest centres in the person and character of its Founder, in the same degree as in Christianity. *Christ is Christianity.* In Him are all its truths, all its motives, all its glory summed up. He is its Alpha and Omega;

the embodiment of all it teaches, all it prescribes, all it promises. In this respect it differs entirely from Mohammedanism, or Buddhism, or any other religion which has largely influenced the world. They rest upon many influences—Christianity rests above all on Christ. It is the spiritual beauty and perfection of His character which has given it the hold it has upon the intelligence of the most intelligent nations of the world—which has given it the sway it has over the most spiritual and exalted souls that have ever lived in the world. The character of Mohammed was by no means an important element, in the influence exercised by his religion. The character of Çakya-Mouni, pure and noble and self-denying as it may have been, was never a living, consistent, and intelligible reality to the millions who submitted themselves to his doctrines or institutions. Both characters may be quite obscured or forgotten, and yet the religions which they founded survive and maintain their force. They are the religions of peoples governed by institutions and traditions, and not by character; by external rather than by moral influences; by the power of will at best, not by the attraction of love. Let it be admitted that there are nations to whom Christianity has also become little more than an external influence —an *institution*—which claims their obedience, rather than a moral power which instinctively sways their hearts—to whom the character of Christ is hidden behind the forms and traditions which have gathered around His name. It remains true, nevertheless, that this character is the great motive power of a living Christianity everywhere, as it was the great motive power of its original progression. And it is no less true that Christianity would wholly fail as a religious influence, were this character to lose its lustre. It does so proportionally, wherever the externalities of the religion darken this spiritual ideal.

Christianity has been the highest spring of human civilization—its most preserving strength. Why so? Because it has given to Humanity a spiritual ideal—a perfect religious conception—which has been the Light of the World. There has been no visible growth in this ideal, and no decay in it. It burst upon the world with a sudden illumination, perfect as it now is. It grew up "occulto velut arbor arvo"—a "root out of a dry ground." In the lapse of ages it has suffered no change, no diminution. Christian creeds have imperfectly defined it; Christian institutions imperfectly represented it; even Christian heroisms have but feebly imitated it. Men and Churches have faintly followed it, and often grossly darkened it by prejudice and passion. But nowhere has there been any advance beyond it. It remains the "Light of the World," as it declared itself to be eighteen centuries ago. Whatever has suffered change, or seems likely to suffer change—whatever revision may await systems or ceremonies, modes of Christian thought or Christian government—this ideal remains lustrous with the same radiance—"the same yesterday, to-day, and for ever"—an example of all love and of all nobleness, of all grace and all true grandeur; inexhaustible in its spiritual fulness, incapable of improvement in its spiritual proportions. Art and life alike, the responsive intellectual and the responsive moral ideal in us, have found in it, and continue to find in it, a perennial fountain of inspiration; they catch some new and higher and more celestial aspects of it; they reach, perhaps, with the deepening thoughtfulness of increasing ages some truer comprehension of it, but the manifoldness of its excellence exceeds all their imitative grasp. It still towers above them, sympathetic at every point to the touch of human aspiration, but out-reaching the highest possibility of human endeavour.

This unexampled ideal and force of character in Jesus is perfectly consistent and intelligible to the Christian. On his theory of the supernatural, or rather his faith in a living God, there is nothing unaccountable in the Christ of the Gospels. The picture only answers to the hand of the Divine Artist. "God manifest in the flesh" could not but present a character unparalleled in spiritual beauty and in capacity of spiritual impulse. Granting the possibility of the supernatural, all follows intelligibly. The Word, "which in the beginning was with God and was God," "was made flesh, and dwelt among us, and we beheld His glory, the glory of the Only Begotten of the Father, full of grace and truth." May we not say that the necessity of the supernatural is already involved in the ideal of the Gospels—the picture which they set before us? It is already there, because *there* is obviously the Divine, "the glory of the Only Begotten of the Father, full of grace and truth;" the perfect spiritual expression which no combination of natural causes could ever yield.

This supernatural origin appears to the Christian the adequate, and the only adequate, explanation of Christ and of Christianity. The cause is equal to the effect—the effect corresponds to the cause; they solve and confirm one another. This has been the unanimous voice of Christendom from the beginning. It is but fair, therefore, to require from one who denies this supernatural origin an adequate and consistent explanation of a fact which has appeared to the general intelligence, as well as to the eye of faith, so clearly to involve the supernatural, and to be unintelligible without it. The fact itself may be denied. The surpassing excellence of the spiritual ideal of the Gospels may be disputed. Infidelity, in order to be consistent, must, perhaps, always in the end take up such a position, and attack the morality, as well as the divinity, of Christ. We shall see how far this is the case with our author. But this is not the ground at first, or indeed mainly, taken up by him. Whatever his treatment of the subject may involve, M. Renan is so far from professing to depreciate the character of Christ, that he is constantly speaking of Him as above every other character; and does not hesitate to say, that "the highest Divine consciousness that ever existed in humanity existed in Him." How does he justify such a view? How does he justify the demands of his subject? Is the character which he has drawn in any degree conformable to them?

I. Jesus, according to him, was the natural offspring of Judaism. He was the incarnation of its moral genius and its Messianic dreams—nothing more. Nature, the teaching of the synagogues, and the enthusiasm of the populace, made Him what He was. Is this possible? Could such a character spring out of such influences, and be produced from such sources? It appears to us wholly impossible. We may allow ever so much for the sweet natural genius and the charming susceptibility of Jesus; but the result is still incredible. For let genius be of the most transcendent order, it must yet connect itself by definite links with its age and time. The most admirable and unique human genius is found to stand in close intellectual and moral relation with its contemporaries. Its growth is understood from what they were, and the influences, direct or indirect, which they exercised upon it. There is in all cases, if not an entirely clear, yet an intelligible affinity, between the highest genius and the tendencies in the midst of which it arose.

This connexion is entirely wanting in the case of Jesus. M. Renan, indeed, talks of moral maxims that were rife in the synagogues, and kindred teachers, such as Hillel and Gamaliel. But his constant affirmations on this subject rest on no evidence, and receive no countenance even from his own detailed explanations. The whole picture of Judaism which he draws is opposed to them. He keeps repeating statements about the moral teaching of the synagogue —statements, let it be remembered, confessedly founded on sources not in existence till two centuries after the Christian era; but he cannot point to any corresponding features in the actual Judaism of the time. The features which this Judaism presented, are sufficiently well known. Pharisaism and Sadduceism represented its two predominant tendencies; and what they were, especially how utterly unmoral they were, no one has better shown than our author. The former had lost the very idea of morality; had obscured and perverted its most obvious and fundamental obligations. A superstitious formalism, consecrating the most frivolous external observances, was its only principle; a baneful and malicious fanaticism its only passion. The Sadducees were without any pretence of spiritual feeling; materialists by profession, ambitious of power, wealth, pleasure, but without a particle of serious thought or sentiment. With both these great parties Christ had confessedly no relations, except those of hostility. It is even a subject of congratulation to M. Renan that his hero, in the progress of his moral development, was so far removed from them—and particularly from Pharisaism, with its solemn, insipid absurdities and hypocrisies—in the quiet villages of Galilee. Here it was in Galilee—in the North—he tells us, that

Jesus imbibed his generous and lofty moral sentiments; and that the inspiring brilliancies of an exquisite nature nurtured and brought to maturity such precious fruit of moral wisdom in Him.

But when we look for any evidence of this moral culture in the north any more than the south—in Galilee any more than in Jerusalem—M. Renan gives us nothing but picturesque description, and dogmatic appeal to the Talmud. He has nowhere vindicated, nowhere even clearly explained, the marked contrast which, according to him, existed between the Judaism of Galilee and of Jerusalem. And for such a contrast there is not the slightest historical foundation. The spirit of the north was of a more free, simple, and natural character; the tendencies of Judaism had not there developed into the same hardened oppositions, the same gross formalism on the one hand, and gross indifference on the other. All that was characteristic in Judaism necessarily reached its most prominent expression in the capital. But withal the Judaism of the north and of the south, of Galilee and of Jerusalem, was substantially the same. So far as the Gospels present a picture of the state of things, it is the same story of partial susceptibility to the higher teaching of Christ, and partial rejection of it, in the north and in the south. The disciples were Galileans. They were, one and all, members of the northern synagogues, and may be taken, from the mere fact of their association with Christ, as above the average examples of the religious and moral spirit which characterized these synagogues. Do they then show, apart from the direct influence and instruction of their Master, any lofty spiritual tendency, any characteristics of spiritual wisdom? Could St. Peter, or even St. John, before the day of Pentecost—when they accompanied our Lord on His Galilean journeys—be conceived as giving utterance to any such sermon as that on the Mount? Is there any indication in them of the same gifts of spiritual wisdom that we find in Him? What capacities of tender and compassionate love there were in St. John, when he received the full unction of the Holy Spirit, his Epistles show. But how different was his original natural Galilean spirit, the spirit which said, "Lord, wilt thou that we command fire to come down from heaven and consume them."[1] This was the spirit of the synagogue, or, at least, a spirit which the teaching of the synagogue had in no

[1] Luke ix. 54.

degree taught John to correct, or even to suspect. If the religious feeling of Galilee had been so much higher than the religious feeling of Jerusalem, would we not have had in the Gospels abundant traces of the fact? If such maxims as compose the Sermon on the Mount had been a common moral currency in the Galilean synagogues, would we not have found some evidence of this in the disciples of our Lord as well as our Lord Himself? Would we not have seen, at least, a higher and more spontaneous susceptibility to His spiritual teaching?

The truth is, that M. Renan has filled up from his own fertile imagination his glowing picture of Galilee. The Galileans were a comparatively rude and simple people: their country was more joyous and fruitful; their cottage-life more sweet, peaceful and idyllic; their habits in all respects more natural. But of a higher spiritual susceptibility, or a richer spiritual wisdom, among them there is no trace. It was at Nazareth, where our Lord "was brought up," that "they rose up and thrust Him out of the city, and led Him unto the brow of the hill whereon their city was built, that they might cast Him down headlong."[1] It was of His native district that He said, "A prophet is not without honour, save in his own country, and in his own house."[2] It was of Capernaum, a town of Galilee, and Chorazin, and Bethsaida, kindred villages, that He laments with such pathetic sadness, that they were utterly indifferent to His teaching; that if the works which had been done in them had been done in Tyre and Sidon, they would long ago have repented.[3]

[1] Luke iv. 29.

[2] Matt. xiii. 57. [3] Luke x. 13—15.

The movement of Judas the Gaulonite or Galilean, so far as it can be taken as an indication of the Galilean spirit, not only shows no countenance to the view of our author, but is entirely opposed to it. Nothing can be conceived more unlike the career of Jesus than the disorderly political aims of this Judas. In Galilee were found, no doubt, the simple Shulamite and the penitent Magdalene, and the good Joseph and Mary; but, side by side, there were also found the political schemer, the dark bigot, the fanatical enthusiast, no less than in Jerusalem. The same variations of natural character, with unimportant modifications, appear in both. In both there is the same mixture of bad and good—of bigotry and simple piety, of insensibility to the truth, and of capacity to receive and obey it. For let it be borne in mind, that if Jerusalem prominently recalls the solemn Pharisee, the cavilling lawyer, and the insipid scribe, there were also found Simeon and Anna; there, or in the immediate neighbourhood, abode Martha and Mary, and Lazarus; there we hear of the inquiring Nicodemus, and the kind and tender Joseph of Arimathea.

In short, M. Renan's elaborate contrast, and the inferences which he founds upon it, have, as we have said, no historical foundation. No more can we conceive Christianity springing up by a natural process of development in Galilee than in Jerusalem. The Spirit of Jesus is as little the spirit of the one as of the other. He found a few congenial souls in both. Probably His early enthusiasm, and the first fresh tenderness of His preaching, encountered a less stern opposition in Galilee than it would have met in Jerusalem, but He owed as little to the one as to the other—to the teachers in the synagogue as to the doctors in the Temple. There were susceptibilities in both to which He addressed Himself; but there was no creative life in either which could have inspired and fashioned Him. The soil was ready here and there in both for the seed of the kingdom; it may have been more ready in the north than the south, but unless the Divine Sower had gone forth to sow, not only would the seed never have germinated to "everlasting life," it would never have been there to touch the receptive soil. The old field of Judaic culture, run to waste through many centuries, and grown over with thorns and briers, might have been turned up many times and slightly fertilised by fresh influences, but it was utterly incapable of nurturing, still more of producing, a new creative germ like Christianity, without the interposition of the Divine Husbandman who originally prepared it. It was, indeed, the prepared field for Christianity. The new germ — "the planting of the Lord and honourable"—needed a fitting soil in which it might "take root downwards, and bear fruit upwards," an Judaism was that soil, divinely pre-arranged. In this sense, Christianity was a development of Judaism, but in no other. The one was the historical preparation for the other when the "fulness of the ages" was come, and the Lord of Life was manifested to destroy the works of evil. Like the block of marble which incloses the living statue, from which the glorious conception of genius is destined to arise with more than mortal intelligence on its radiant form and countenance, Judaism may be said to have inclosed Christianity, and to have formed the material out of which it was hewn; but no more than the blind amorphous mass can grow spontaneously into living outline and exquisite expression, could the shapeless chaos of Jewish notions eighteen centuries ago have grown into the living Gospel.

M. Renan is, indeed, forced upon this conclusion against his will. Under the mere pressure of the facts, he is driven to recognise in Jesus a living creative genius entirely differing from anything in Judaism.[1] Neither here, nor anywhere, is he very careful of consistency, trusting to the facile resources of his brilliant rhetoric. On the one hand he tells us that in the early teaching of Jesus there is nothing

[1] Pp. 74—77.

with which the synagogue was not already familiar. Soon afterwards he enlarges upon the splendid originality of Jesus in His conception of God as a Father—as "our Father in Heaven." "This is His grand act of originality; in this He owes nothing to His race. Neither Jew nor Mussulman has ever understood this delightful theology of Love. The God of Jesus is no fatal Master, who kills us when He pleases, condemns us when He pleases, saves us when He pleases. The God of Jesus is our Father. He is the God of humanity."[1] M. Renan is here perfectly right. This revelation of the Fatherhood of God is the great act of originality in Jesus—the great discovery of Christianity. No human religion had dreamed of it, no human philosophy announced it, and both had done all that they

[1] Pp. 74—77.

ever could do for the world before the advent of Christianity. The conception of God as infinitely great and holy, yet infinitely tender and merciful—as doing according to His will among the armies of heaven and the inhabitants of the lower world, and yet ordering all things with unerring righteousness and careful love—as utterly removed from all earthly contact, and yet not suffering a sparrow to fall to the ground without His permission, or hearing unheeded the humblest cry of His creatures—as enthroned in inaccessible light which no man can approach unto, and yet very near to us even in our hearts—this sublime conception, which the world confessedly owes to Christianity, is of itself sufficient to demonstrate the divine originality of Jesus. Human thought had not only failed to elaborate it, the highest of the schools not only been unable to seize it with any clearness or consistency of vision, but to this day, wherever it turns from the light of Christianity, human thought fails to preserve the great conception, and erects in its stead some barren idol—the Eternal Process of Hegel, or the mute unconscious Law of Renan.

The Christ of the Gospels, then, is unintelligible on M. Renan's principles. There is really no foundation for the character which he has drawn. The origin of Christianity cannot be explained even by the most favourable concurrence of natural causes in Galilee eighteen centuries ago. Nature may do much for a responsive soul, but even its most glorious combinations have in themselves no creative effect. Sweet genius, and a charming spiritual susceptibility may constitute an attractive character, and even rise to a height of powerful and commanding influence in dealing with current spiritual influences, moving all minds, and awaiting only some kindling touch to come forth into permanent activity. This is the obvious secret of such characters as St. Francis of Assisi, and others. Marvellous as their career and the power which they exercised may be, we understand them readily, because we see the conditions out of which they sprang. But these conditions we nowhere see in the case of Jesus. Let nature and genius have all the effect that can be ascribed to them, they have nowhere produced such a character; they have in no case—not even in one memorable case which will occur to most minds, that of Socrates, —approximated to the production of such a character; they have nowhere developed into such an originality of spiritual conception, nor moulded into such a perfect proportion of spiritual greatness. No mere human influences have ever germinated into such a consummate expression of wisdom and love, of "grace and truth." The loftiest human model still stands—with its strange mixture of loftiness and lowness, of Divine light and human darkness, of righteousness of aim and error of practice—at an infinite distance. Nor was this model, be it remembered, the production of Jewish soil and of an effete age.

The more all the characteristics of the Judaism of the first century are studied, the more all the tendencies of the time are investigated, the more impossible will it appear that they could have given birth to such a life as Christ's and such a doctrine as Christianity. It might even be said, that of all the spiritual forces then at work in the world, Judaism really seems the less capable of originating such a life and such a doctrine. It is not merely a higher spirit which breathes in the Gospel, but it is a *different* spirit, a spirit which in its creative breadth and life absorbs every other and entirely transforms it. This new *creative* energy, manifesting in contact with Judaism and Hellenism, and every prevailing form of faith, a new plastic life, is the characteristically Divine element of Christianity; and in this respect it is unlike every system and every religion of the time.

The case of Philo, to which our author so often alludes, presents here an instructive contrast. In the writings of the Alexandrian Jewish philosopher, there are many impressive gleams of a lofty moral doctrine; there is especially the same constant recognition of a higher rational and spiritual life, and the worthlessness, in comparison, of the mere material and sensitive life,[1] that we find in the Gospels and also in Socrates; there are comprehensive views of God; but there is no creative, spiritual conception, fusing all together, and combining them into a living doctrine, capable of animating men's hearts, controlling their principles, and guiding their conduct. The finest spiritual thoughts are mixed up with the most fantastic intellectual and spiritual conceits; glimpses of truth are obscured by shadows of error, visions of a living God by suspicions of a mere universal principle,[2] removed beyond all human contact and sympathy.

And the very same, and in a still higher

[1] See Quis Rerum. Div. Heres? 8 et seq. iii. Ed. Tauchnitz. I have only recently made any study of Philo, and therefore speak from a partial knowledge. But I do not think any candid student of Philo and the Gospels will dispute the representation of the text.

[2] Philo (Mangey's Edit.) I. 560, 582, &c.

degree, is notoriously true of the moral doctrine of the Talmud. Did we grant all that our author says of the excellence of its moral precepts, and their coincidence with those of the Gospel; did we grant even that which would be quite unwarrantable, the higher originality of the Talmudical precepts; he would be far from making out his point. For these precepts are, in the Talmud, embedded amidst a mass of absurdities of the most frivolous and debasing description; immoral in principle and ridiculous in end. Now this is a difference not merely in degree, but in kind; a difference which settles the whole question, and leaves the divine originality of the Gospels as conspicuous as ever. For no intelligent student has ever claimed absolute originality for every precept of the Gospels; no one has denied, or need deny, that the sayings of

Christ in the Sermon on the Mount, and elsewhere, may have been partly derived and adapted from Jewish sources (although this has actually not been proved), and may therefore be paralleled by similar sayings in the Talmud. Every one has recognised with a delightful satisfaction the striking coincidence between some of these sayings, and those of the Platonic Socrates.[1] But no such manifest coincidence, no such indebtedness, even could it be proved, touches the essential originality of the evangelical doctrine. This consists, above all, in the completeness of that doctrine, and its unity of creative conception and force. There are no shadows and no reserves in it, no painful gropings or hesitations, no uncertainties;

[1] See among other examples of this, Plato, Legg. 5, 742 e.; Gorg. 507 b.; Rep. 8, 555 c.; and 9, 591 e.; and 9, 586 a.; Tim. 28 c. 37, c.; Theact. 176 a.; Apol. 29 b.

but all is clear, comprehensive, axiomatic, vitally organized and rounded into a perfect harmony; simple, so that any child may understand it, yet subtle and profound enough to satisfy the deepest gaze of the philosopher. There may be analogous precepts in other religions, but there is no such *religious system* anywhere, nor any approach to it. Other ages of the world have had their great teachers; fragments of the highest truth may be gathered from many sources; but no age has had a Teacher such as Galilee had in the first century; and no such living and fertile unity of doctrine has ever been made known to the world.

II. But the Christ of the Gospels is not only unintelligible on M. Renan's data; the portrait which he has drawn is, moreover, inconsistent in itself. The ideal which he paints is contradictory and incredible. To the Christian the character of Christ is at once intelligible in its origin, and perfectly consistent in its twofold activity, moral and miraculous, "God manifest in the flesh" could not but be both infinitely beautiful in character and miraculous in working. A supernatural Personality was only manifesting itself according to its proper nature, in the exhibition of supernatural powers of healing, and of raising the dead. Such miracles as fill the Gospels, not only do not contradict the idea of such a personality, but form its fitting, and, so to speak, necessary witness. The strange thing would have been if such a Personality had not wrought such miracles; for how otherwise could the supernatural bear witness to itself save in manifestations of supernatural love and power?

The mere idea of wonder-working for the sake of *éclat*, or the gratification of personal distinction, is utterly alien to the character of the Christian miracles. They are never artistically prepared, they are not preluded by any self-assertion; audiences are not assembled to witness them; but they come forth as the proper effluence of the Divine Man when He walks the earth. At the very commencement of His ministry, in the Synagogue of Capernaum, in the house of a newly-married friend in Cana of Galilee—so soon as the time was come, when He must be about His Father's business and accomplish the works that had been given Him to do, His miraculous powers manifest themselves. So far from being factitious inventions to secure reputation, or to preserve what reputation He had already acquired, they are the actual, the spontaneous, expression of the Mind and Spirit that were in Him; for those who saw them were all amazed, and spake among themselves, saying, "*What a word is this!* for with authority and power He commandeth the unclean spirits, and they come out."[1]

There is, therefore, to the Christian a perfect consistency between the character and the works of Christ. To M. Renan they are utterly inconsistent, and he is condescending enough to propose *excuses* for the Evangelical miracles. "It is necessary," he says, "to admit that some acts, which our enlightened age must regard as displays of illusion or madness, occupy a chief place in the life of Jesus.[2] But an apology may be found for them in the consideration that all popular heroes and reformers were then expected to work mira-

[1] Luke iv. 36. [2] P. 266.

cles. *Thaumaturgy* was a *rôle* of the time from which no great man could escape. The school of Alexandria was a noble school, and yet it was devoted to practices of extravagant theurgy. Socrates and Pascal were not exempt from hallucinations." How then can we expect Jesus to be singular in this respect? In the direct face of all evidence it is asserted that Jesus assumed with reluctance the thaumaturgic *rôle*. It was unknown to the first beautiful and joyous period of His life—the period of His fresh, moral enthusiasm in Galilee, and the Sermon on the Mount; and it was only assumed when He saw symptoms of His influence beginning to wane, and when the opposition which He encountered kindled in Him a more stormy zeal. To the last it was uncongenial to Him. "He was a thaumaturgist and an exorcist in spite of Himself."

Not to insist upon the total lack of evidence for such an account of Christ's miracles, or rather the abounding evidence against it, such a character as M. Renan thus attributes to Jesus, is plainly self-contradictory. It is impossible to conceive such a union of moral excellence with such thaumaturgic imposture as he attributes to Him. Men of the highest goodness may no doubt fall into grave mistakes. Pascal may believe in the miracle of the Holy Thorn; and a St. Bernard and St. Francis may delude themselves, in special moments of spiritual access, with the possession of miraculous powers. But there is nothing really parallel in such cases to the miraculous career of Jesus. None of these men claimed, in the sense that He did, a supernatural mission. Even assuming their own point of view, the miraculous was at the most an accident in their lives. But it *was the characteristic life* of Jesus; no after-thought, no concession forced upon him, but the primary and appropriate manifestation of His Messianic mission, and the self-constituted vindication of the Divinity which He claimed. It is impossible to apologize for such a miraculous career,—for such miraculous claims,—supposing them to have been factitious and assumed. If Jesus was, according to M. Renan, a mere wonder-worker, a thaumaturgist, like Apollonius of Tyana, He could not be the noble and beautiful character which he describes. The Preacher on the Mount would cry shame upon the thaumaturgist in Capernaum, in Cana, in Nain. Character, in this strange world of ours, is often mysteriously complex; the good and the evil lying side by side, in startling and perplexing combination; but the mournfullest contradictions of character that the world has ever witnessed, would be outrivalled by the contradiction which the character of Christ would thus present. The "highest consciousness of God that has ever existed in the bosom of humanity," allied to the tricks of the wonder-worker, the impostures of the exorcist—who does not feel his spirit shudder at such a thought? who does not feel, at such a suggestion, the shadows of the world's mystery to darken over him, and the idea of the Divine to go out of his heart in the blackness of an inexplicable confusion? Mixed as are the representations of human history, and strangely combined as are the possibilities of good and evil in many a soul, such an association as that of imposture with the name of Jesus, exceeds all the limits of human credibility.

The old infidelity, which was audacious to deny any Divine excellence to Christ, which would have repudiated as superstitious the concession of M. Renan, that He had the highest consciousness of the Divine, was, in reality, more consistent than this new infidelity. It hated the Gospel, and it called Christ deliberately an impostor. It recognised nothing Divine, nothing good in Him; and so, at least, it was consistent as it was audacious. Historical criticism has driven such an infidelity out of the field. It is nowhere to be found now, save in the ranks of ignorance and irreligion. The character of Christ, in all moral attributes, reveals itself the greater, the more it is studied in the full light, and by the higher methods, of modern historical inquiry. M. Renan is forced, amidst all his inconsistencies, to admire its surpassing excellence—its divine beauty. It appears to us impossible to do this, and yet to deny the supernatural claims of Christ. His morality and His miracles are inseparably bound up together, the complementary attributes of the same Divine Personality. The critical solvents which avail in other cases do not avail here. It is possible, for example, to recognise with the modern spirit of historical inquiry the genuine greatness of Mahomet, and the species of divine enthusiasm, so to speak, which carried him forward in his marvellous career. It is possible in his case to do this, and at the same time to deny to him any supernatural or divine mission; for he did not claim to be himself endowed with miraculous powers—he did not appeal to the works which he did as attestation of his divine mission—he did not, in fact, profess to work miracles;

although he professed to be the "prophet" of God, and to hold special communications with heaven. He claimed merely what many enthusiasts have claimed — what Socrates claimed, what Cromwell claimed; and the historical sense is not offended in recognising even the moral greatness of such characters, while questioning the reality of their supposed divine communications. An exalted enthusiasm, frequently losing itself in the Divine, explains all, or nearly all. The same is true of such characters as St. Francis of Assisi, Joan of Arc, and others which M. Renan uses as parallels.

But it is impossible to place Christ on the level of such characters, and to explain His career on the same principles, And for the simple reason, that the supernatural in His case is no mere temporary access of divine enthusiasm; no possible self-creation of a divine madness in the brain; it is the sphere in which He lives; it is the constant manifestation of His activity; it is the test of His mission clearly recognised and urged by Himself. Let any one only take up the Gospel of St. Matthew—we appeal to it because M. Renan so uniformly appeals to it, and professes to put it above the others—and notice how the very commencement of our Lord's ministry[1] witnesses itself in a cluster of miraculous acts. The hour of His divine manifestation is come, and this shows itself in an outburst of supernatural love and power: cleansing the leper, healing the sick, stilling the tempest, casting out devils, raising the dead, restoring sight to the blind and speech to the dumb. As He Himself said,

[1] Matt. viii. 9.

when the imprisoned Baptist sent his disciples to make sure anew whether He was the Messiah, or whether they should look for another: "The blind receive their sight, and the lame walk, the lepers are cleansed, the deaf hear, the dead are raised up, and the poor have the Gospel preached to them." These acts were not accidents in His career, but "mighty works," wrought with a conscious aim, and to which He constantly appealed.

There can be only one possible explanation of miraculous claims such as these, consistently with the honesty of the person who makes them, viz. their reality. The idea of mere enthusiasm, or of lofty self-exaltation, will in no degree explain them. From such enthusiasm, indeed; from anything of that divine madness—that sibylline rapture which is the recognised attribute of the ordinary prophetic enthusiast—the character of Christ is singularly free. Its type is that of serene majesty, of calmly-conscious, clear, profound, stedfast intelligence, in which the Divine is mirrored with pellucid consistency. The historical sense, therefore, at once rejects the idea of ranking such a character with any of those that have been mentioned. Its canons of explanation fail here. The moral purity of such a character can only be vindicated in combination with the reality of the divine acts which illustrated it. If Jesus was a true man—still more, a man in whom the divine consciousness was more than in any other man—He was also Divine; for He wrought the works of God, and these works bore witness to Him that He came from God, and that God was in Him.

There are other points of view in which

this argument of consistency might be urged, and in a very striking manner. We only allude to one more at present. The modern theory of Christ's character, by those who deny His divinity, is that of a great religious hero and martyr; one who died to vindicate human liberty, and the right of spiritual intelligence against the oppression of priestcraft and the servilities of a godless material power. This is so far the view of our author. In the closing period of His career, Christ is to him something of such a hero and martyr. But he is conscious also how imperfectly such a character fits Christ, and especially the Christ of the Passion. There is a feeling, scarcely of awe—for that could not be—but of softened solemnity, that moves even his pages, as he recounts the story of the Passion. And what a story is that!

What a picture of infinite, mysterious sorrow!—of shadow deeper than all other shadow that has ever lain on our earth!—as Jesus withdrew from His disciples "about a stone's cast," and fell on His face and prayed, saying, "O my Father, if it be possible, let this cup pass from Me; nevertheless, not as I will, but as Thou wilt." How does the soul go forth in ineffable tenderness towards the Bearer of such a burden as bowed the Son of Man to the earth; when His spirit groaned in incomprehensible travail, and "the sweat was as it were great drops of blood falling down to the ground." But is this the characteristic spirit of the hero and martyr? Do we feel, as we read the story of the Passion, that we are contemplating merely the struggles of a great human soul? Is that "agony and bloody sweat," that cry of impassioned mystery, that weakness and shrinking as from death, and, finally, that horror of great darkness as He hung upon the cross, and felt that God had forsaken Him,—is all this of the nature of heroic martyrdom? Is it not something entirely different from the stedfast rejoicing willingness of a Paul: "I am ready to be offered up, and the time of my departure is at hand"? from the blind headlong rapture of an Ignatius: "Suffer me to be the food of wild beasts; do not intercede for me. Fire and the cross, the assaults of wild beasts, the tearing of my limbs, the breaking of my bones, the grinding of my whole body—I welcome them all"?[1] Assuredly it is. As we stand in spirit by the side of the sleeping disciples and watch their suffering Lord; as we hear Him cry from the cross, "My God,

[1] Ignatii Epist. ad Romanos, c. 4, 5.

My God, why hast Thou forsaken Me," before He bowed His head and gave up the ghost; we feel we are entering into the communion of a deeper and more mysterious sorrow than the world has ever known —a sorrow which is not weakness—a sorrow in which no notes of mere martyr-triumph mingle, which no gleam of rejoicing heroism illumines, but which becomes bright with an awful meaning, then and only then, when we recognise in it the reality of a Divine Sacrifice for the sins of the world; the offering up of Him, who "though He knew no sin, yet was made sin for us, that we might be made the righteousness of God in Him."

III. But, finally, the portrait which M. Renan has given us in his volume is not only unintelligible and inconsistent, but moreover inadequate. It fails to explain the effects which have followed from the character and doctrines of Christ. These effects have always been considered as a legitimate evidence of the Divine origin of Christianity. Nothing but a Divine Power, it has been argued, could originate such a world-transforming influence as Christianity; and the argument is perfectly valid in the view of what we have said; viz. that Christianity has spread, and continues to spread, mainly by virtue of its spiritual attractiveness. It was the Divine life—the moral might in it—which first subdued the Roman world, and then moulded into new and higher forms of civilization the northern races that overspread it, and have since developed into the great European nations. By the same means it continues to this day to move these nations and the wide-spreading nationalities that have sprung from them in other hemispheres; to colour and exalt all their highest thoughts and all their social and legislative activities. Not only so; but gradual, and even here and there reactionary, as may seem the course of missionary enterprise, Christianity continues to manifest throughout the world, and, in contact with other religions, a spiritually subduing and transforming force, which is altogether unparalleled. Unlike other religions—particularly those great Eastern religions, whose spread and power, in point of mere magnitude, present the only parallel to it— it radiates from the highest centres of human intelligence, carrying with it not merely a new faith, but the highest attributes of intelligence wherever it penetrates. Other religions radiate from centres of comparative ignorance, and show themselves utterly powerless in contact with the awakened energies of humanity in other regions. Christianity remains the only vitalizing spiritual power in the world; and apart from the living energy that lies in it, it may be doubtful whether there is any reality of moral progress in the world. Thought and science, with all their advances, would prove but poor factors in this progress, were it not for the impulses which they borrow from Christian philanthropy and enterprise.

And all this sum of spiritual influence our author supposes to have sprung from a man, half enthusiast, half charlatan—a man himself, indeed, of the noblest spiritual impulses, and the highest divine consciousness, but who yet condescended to spread his doctrine by falsehood, and to excite attention by artifices and imposture! This

Jesus whom M. Renan pictures beside the grave of Lazarus, half the dupe and half the impostor in the disgraceful scene—*He* is to be conceived as standing at the head of this unexampled moral development of humanity! It is all the result of the fine thoughts and beautiful sentiments which He promulgated. This is not merely our way of putting it—M. Renan distinctly claims for the Jesus whom he has described such an unexampled influence. "Christianity," he says, in his concluding chapter, "has become almost synonymous with religion. Apart from the great and good Christian tradition we should know nothing of religion. It would be mere barrenness. Jesus has founded religion in humanity, as Socrates has founded in it philosophy, and Aristotle science. Since Socrates and Aristotle, philosophy and science have made immense progress; but all has been built upon the foundations which they laid. In the same manner, before Jesus, religious thought had passed through many revolutions. Since Jesus it has made great conquests; but we have not left behind, we shall never leave behind, the essential idea which Jesus created. He has fixed for ever the idea of pure worship. In this sense His religion is without limits. The Church has had its epochs, its phases; its symbols, which have been, or will be, but temporary; but Jesus has founded absolute religion, excluding nothing, defining nothing, save only the sentiment."[1]

This religion of humanity—the only religion worthy of man, or having any elements of permanence in it—has yet been founded

[1] Pp. 445-46. "N'excluant rien, ne déterminant rien, si ce n'est le sentiment."

in imposture! Is this conceivable? Is it not utterly incredible? Many powers have moved the world, and left tracks of light behind them on its darkened history. As we look back upon them, we are forced to recognise the strange mixture of the evil with the good which they present. They are of the world, and we are not surprised to find the taint of the world's error—it may be of the world's vice—upon them. But here is a power which has moved the world to unexampled good—which in itself, and so far as it has been unspoiled by other admixture, has shone with a stainless lustre upon all the world's darkness; and we are to believe that not only error, but falsehood has mingled in its origin? Say what we will of the difference of the oriental nature, of its incapacity of distinguishing truth from falsehood in our European sense—is it not mockery in such a case to urge such palliations, or to suppose that they have any application?[1] The world has been regenerated. Christendom, with its beautiful sanctities, its blessed charities, its wise and beneficent institutes, its peaceful and glorious aspirations, has been created. The Temple of Humanity—all that is high, and pure, and noble in human thought and feeling and enterprise—has been built upon "the foundation of apostles and prophets—Jesus Christ the chief corner stone." And yet we are to suppose that delusion—that falsehood lies below all this, that the Incarnation is a dream, the Resurrection a legend? May we not say, without exaggeration, that the difficulties of unbelief are far greater than those of faith—that it makes in the end demands upon our understanding far more importunate and amazing?

[1] P. 252.

Infidelity, in the course of its rapid developments in recent years, seems to make this more and more apparent. And it is well that it should do so. Deplorable as are the wounds which it inflicts upon many hearts and consciences, it is better that it should have in this way its perfect work—better far, certainly, than that it should experience any material checks, or be met by other arguments than those of reason and faith, in that great and apparently progressive conflict between truth and error, which God has seen meet to suffer in the world. The truth, as Milton long ago said, has no need to fear, save when other weapons than its own are employed in its defence. "If my kingdom were of this world, then would my servants fight. But now is my kingdom not from hence. To this end was I born, and for this came

I into the world, that I should bear witness of the Truth." The truth is everywhere and in all ages its own witness. It fights with its own weapons, which are never the weapons of material force, of social persecution, or of official penalties. These only degrade and weaken it. In itself alone, in its own intrinsic rationality and spiritual consistency and influence, it is eternally strong, "sharp and powerful as any two-edged sword, piercing to the dividing asunder of soul and spirit, of the joints and marrow,— a discoverer of the thoughts and intents of the heart." It will never fail to vindicate this strength sooner or later against any attack, however subtle or strong, that may be directed against it.

There have been attacks made upon it, and there may still be attacks made upon it, far more formidable than the "Vie de

Jésus" of M. Renan. But there has been seldom any book which has put the issue between Christianity and Unbelief more plainly than this one. Whatever be M. Renan's defects, there can be no doubt that he has set forth in a singularly direct, perspicuous and intelligible form, the great historical problem of the origin of Christianity. If he is wanting in the gravity and scientific earnestness of the German theologians, he is also free from their pseudo-abstractions, and the vague generalities in which they so often lose themselves and weary the world. The problem is reduced by him to its naked historical aspects. That he has failed in working it out from his point of view, notwithstanding all his resources of learning and literary art—failed historically to render any adequate, consistent, or satisfactory account of the origin of Christianity and of the character of its great Founder, is negatively one of the strongest testimonies to its Divine origin that could have been given. For this is the only historical alternative that remains. If Christianity be not of the Jews, of whom concerning the flesh Christ came; if it be not a natural product of Judaism; it is from God directly and extraordinarily, a living seed planted by the Divine hand, and growing up into all the fair proportions of Faith, Hope, and Charity, with which it has blessed and beautified the world.

THE END.

CPSIA information can be obtained
at www.ICGtesting.com
Printed in the USA
LVHW092304230322
714114LV00005BA/185

9 783752 582543